CHAPTER ON

CH00393683

Ex Royal Marine Commando, Clive Nixon, or
rather surprised when the phone rang so late
Answering with his usual, "hello Nick", he was
the voice of Arthur, his longtime friend and col
the nickname of "the fixer" earned for his methods of always organising, or
fixing events for his comrades on duty all over the world, more recently in Iraq
and Afghanistan.

Clive had neither seen nor heard from Arthur for about two years, since they
both left the forces and entered civvy street, despite their promises to keep in
touch.

"Fancy a get together" asked Arthur, "a bit of a bender just the four of us. You,
me, taff and the Prince."

"Are you kidding ? Where the hell are you?"

"Me and taff are in a hotel about five miles from you, and the Prince will be
here tomorrow from Surrey."

"So where's the meet ?

"Do you know the White Lion at Swynnerton ?"

"Yes of course, the landlords a mate. I've had a few lock-ins there over the
years."

"That's fixed then, nineteen hundred hours tomorrow. The four of us back
together again, the world had better watch out eh?"

"Terrific, but whats the occasion" enquired Nick.

"Do we need one? Just thought that we ought to keep in touch" retorted Arthur.

"See you all tomorrow night then, cheers for now, mention my name to Len, the
landlord, he'll probably give you a discount."

"Already have" replied the fixer.

Replacing the handset, Nick opened the fridge and took out a cold can of
beer, pulled the ringtop and poured the contents into his favourite handled glass,
a present from his son Tony on his last birthday.

He stepped outside into the garden, lit a cigarette and began to drink his beer. It
was late July and the neat flowerbeds his wife Tanya had planted were still in
bloom, giving off a pleasant scent. The lawn was quite a vivid green after all the
rain and in need of a trim, a job he had got planned for tomorrow morning. He
took a long hard drag on his cigarette, blowing the exhaled smoke into the night
sky, twinkling stars illuminating the almost black beyond. His thoughts were
very deep. Downing his beer, he sighed a very long sigh, reliving times that had
passed, times that he fondly remembered, but mostly times that he would rather
not recall and preferred to condemn to the past. As lovely as it was to hear
Arthur's voice again, and the prospect of seeing him, Taff and the Prince after

all this time was very appealing, he worried a bit about re-igniting some of the bad memories.

For the last two years Nick had led a fairly subdued life in comparison to his previous twelve in the commandos. He had taken on a job as a security manager, looking after four sites of a motor car retailing operation in the Potteries and had four staff to control. The job bored him to tears, but it paid the bills and more importantly allowed him to spend quality time with his gorgeous wife Tanya and his two sons, Tony aged twelve and ten year old Craig. The fifth member of his family was Major, a german shepherd he had raised from a pup.

His ambition was to get his lads through school and college or university and then fulfil his dream of running his own country pub. Having spent many years on the customer side of the bar, he often visualised himself on the other side as mine host. A chocolate box style country inn with a roaring log fire in the winter, providing a warm welcome to the local villagers, enjoying a drink and some banter with his patrons.

A lovely beer garden next to a river, set out with solid furniture and a child's play area. Quite skilled in the kitchen, Nick would often rustle up some very tasty morsels for the family and quite fancied the idea of providing good quality meals for his customers. His pipedream had been in his mind for some years and gave him the strength to persevere during those trying years fighting the Taliban.

Major, the alsation, ambled out of the kitchen and deliberately nudged Nick as if to say, "Its time for my walk." His dark brown eyes looked at his master, waiting patiently for a sign from him, who seemed to be a million miles away. Nick took a deep draw on his cigarette and blew three perfect smoke rings into the air, one for each of his comrades. He reached down and patted Major gently on his black and gold shoulders.

Taking another sip from his glass he sat on the wooden bench underneath the kitchen window. The dog sat on Nicks feet, his back straight as a die, his noble head held high and put a paw on Nick's knee. Memories of his time in Afghanistan flooded back. Comrades, Arthur, the fixer, a fairly quiet unassuming type of guy, sporting a full set (beard and tash), a bit of a beer belly, that he insisted was bought and paid for, who had a penchant for always getting things done. No matter what the obstacle he seemed to have a knack of finding a solution and often cajoled people into helping without them realizing what he was doing. He was a very loyal man, valuing his friends and their friendship. Being an only child he only ever knew the closeness of his comrades, they were his "family", his confidantes and the people he loved most in the world.

Taff, alias Rhys Llewellyn made up the third of this intrepid foursome. A Welshman from the Valleys just north of Swansea. built like a Tank, Taff embodied the typical traditional Welshman. He played semi professional rugby before joining up. His ambition was to emulate his father who had been a marine for twenty two years, and had been decorated several times for bravery. Sadly he

2

had succumbed to cancer at the age of forty one when Rhys was only fourteen years old.

Taff became very strong and very tough at a relatively young age, caring for his mum and younger sister Megan. Two days after his eighteenth birthday his mother passed away, Megan went to live with his aunt and he entered the forces.

The Prince, real name Charles Royal, came from a very well to do family who lived in Surrey. His father was a dentist with a very lucrative practice and his mother owned a successful boutique in the most fashionable part of town, importing from China, and supplying the affluent gullables at over inflated prices, securing good profits. Educated at Oxford the Prince yearned for adventure, having led a stifled life at home and against his parents wishes he joined the forces.

At first he struggled a bit with the others, they perceived him to be privileged coming from such a background, but in truth he was a very down to earth, ordinary caring person. To a degree he was a little jealous of some of his comrades who came from large, loving families. He felt that he had missed out a bit during his childhood listening to some of the lads dits (stories) about their home lives.

He overcompensated by being a really true friend, someone you could rely upon one hundred percent when the chips were down. His true forte was shooting. A crack shot, he won every competition he had ever entered. Standing six feet tall and very handsome he'd had a string of lady friends over the years, but never yet found the perfect lady.

Nick imbibed a long deep lungful of the cool night air, winked at the stars, and stepped back into the kitchen. Major whimpered at him "OK then. Come on, lets go around the block" he conceded. Majors tail wagging heralded some freedom. Upon their return the dog drank from his bowl and settled down for the night.

Locking everywhere up and switching off the lights Nick quietly went upstairs. He gently pushed open Tony's bedroom door and peered in. His son was fast asleep. Pulling the door to, he checked on Craig, the youngest. His bedside light was on and his music system was still playing. Nick switched things off and carefully pulled the duvet over his sleeping son.

In the bathroom Nick stared into the mirror and looked back at himself. For some reason he felt a bit of a failure. It seemed as though he had achieved so much in a relatively short space of time in the Marines, had risen through the ranks and then just accepted this menial job in civvy street. He lacked excitement, the blood rush of combat. Not suffering from all these modern illnesses of post conflict stress. It felt the complete opposite.

The stress was to contend with this mundane existence.

His son Tony was so keen at sport and just loved to run. Cross country, one hundred metres, four hundred metres, even the mile. His lad was so fit it made

Nick feel out of breath just thinking about it. Youngest Craig, was almost the complete opposite. A bit of a homebird but so very accomplished on the guitar. He spent most evenings practicing and would sometimes try to sing. His granddad, Nick's father, used to sing in his local pub, especially after a few bevies, so perhaps the genes had travelled.

He went into their bedroom where his wife Tanya was sleeping soundly. Her golden hair stretched across the pillow, highlighting the beauty of her high cheek bones, silky smooth skin and adorable face. Married for fourteen years, Nick felt privileged to be so well blessed with such a gorgeous wife. Sitting very gently on the bed beside her, Nick carefully stroked her hair and tenderly planted a peck on her forehead. Momentarily her breathing altered and she snuggled deeply into the white fresh linen pillowcase. Nick slid quietly under the covers and placed his arm around her, reassuringly. He was so looking forward to meeting his three 'bezzy oppos' from the Marines again tomorrow, but he knew that Tanya may not be quite as enthusiastic about it.

CHAPTER TWO

As though he had a built in alarm clock, Nick woke at his usual time, six am, and without disturbing Tanya, slipped quietly out of bed and into the bathroom. Shaved and showered, he dressed casually to enjoy his weekend off, without his security uniform.

Downstairs, Major was waiting in anticipation of his early morning jaunt with his master. Nick drank some fresh grapefruit juice and took the dogs lead from it's hook on the back door, prompting a tail wag strong enough to knock anyone off their feet standing too close. The pair set off and as usual, Nick bimbled along the street allowing his canine friend to sniff his immediate territory, but once they had rounded the corner, passed the church, and entered the park, he set off at a cracking pace, Major having to run hard to keep up.

Life as a bootneck (Royal Marine) had taught him so much about fitness, though not exactly fanatical, he took pride in his body and regularly exercised. After a couple of miles through the park, the pair slowed to more of a gentle jog. Back home, Nick refreshed the dogs water bowl and fed him. Major wolfed the lot and went into the garden.

Despite his love of fitness, Nick's weakness was his love of cigarettes, borne out of a lot of factors in his life. The habit that he inwardly detested in himself, but took comfort from, and persisted in. A vice that, for the time being at least, he would allow himself to continue enjoying. Lighting one he stepped into the garden and watched the sunrise brightening the sky giving hope for a lovely day. Major lay quite still on the grass, panting a little, but content after his run out and breakfast.

Ordinarily Nick would insist that his two lads, cleaned and polished their own shoes over the weekend, but on this occasion, he did them himself. Gleaming, he placed the immaculate footwear neatly side by side. Perhaps subconsciously he was currying favour, to lessen the impact of telling the family that he was going to have a night out with his old mates from his former life.

Preparing the table for breakfast Nick accidentally knocked a family photograph off the sideboard. It fell to the laminated floor with a crash. He picked it up. The glass on the front of the frame was fragmented with the segments of glass arcing from the corner, almost obliterating the faces of Tanya, Tony and Craig.

His own face was still perfectly visible through a larger unbroken segment of glass. It was one of Tanya's favourite family snapshots taken when Nick came home, having left the Marines. Nick popped it into a drawer, thinking to get it repaired and put back before anyone noticed.

He continued with the breakfast preparations, a full English to set them all up for the day. The aroma of sizzling bacon aroused the lads and they bounded down the stairs breaking the silence Nick had enjoyed so far. With their usual exuberant banter each one taunted the other about yesterday's exam results. On the whole neither had done badly but both could have done better. Tony had only managed second place in the 400 metres in the school sports, and Craig had failed his part two guitar exam.

"Hey you two calm down a bit, your mother's having a lie in!" commanded Nick.

"It's ok dad, she's in the shower," excused Tony.

"Even so, you two need to keep it down a bit, go play football with the dog and I'll call you when breakfast is ready."

Nick continued and produced a fantastic breakfast with every conceivable ingredient. Right on cue Tanya appeared in the kitchen wearing a bathrobe, her hair still wet from the shower, sidled up behind the chef, gave him a big squeeze round the waist from behind, and said "Something smells very nice," Turning his head to one side he puckered his lip and on tip toes, Tanya reached up to give him a kiss, "and you're not bad either" she finished.

Smiling his usual loving, cheery smile Nick said "Have a seat madam, breakfast is served."

Nick tapped on the kitchen window and beckoned the two lads to come in. Placed before them was a magnificent mouth watering full English with the fluffiest, bright yellow, chunky scrambled eggs, surrounding the tastiest lean thick bacon with baked beans, fresh tomatoes and his coup de gras, melted cheese filled mushrooms and lots of well done toast.

With clean plates all round, Tanya asked, "So what are we going to do today then?"

The lads fancied the latest film at the cinema, but Nick dismissed that idea saying that they could go to see films on cold, wet days.

"What about the park? We could take a boat out" he suggested.

With some rather insipid agreement the day was decided. Being a bit of a stickler, a legacy of his training and lifestyle, Nick insisted that the lads were dressed accordingly. Tanya did likewise, although she would look a million dollars in a bin bag.

Arriving at the park Nick tethered Major to the fence next to the boat hire jetty. The family took a rowing boat out onto the lake, Nick doing the initial rowing. Despite two years in civvy street away from the rigours of naval life, he had always kept himself in pretty good shape.

Flexing his muscles he pulled the oars through the water with apparent ease, propelling the little wooden number seven across the lake at a reasonable rate of knots. The midday sunshine glistened on the beads of sweat forming on his bald head. Whenever challenged about his lack of follicles he had a stock answer. God made some beautiful heads, the rest he covered with hair.

Reaching a small wooded island in the middle of the lake, Nick moored the boat momentarily and swapped places with the lads. They now had an oar each and Nick sat in the bow with Tanya. Nick removed his jacket, revealing a tattoo on his right forearm, saying 'It's a state of mind', the watchword of the Royal

Marine Commandos. His left forearm had a Commando Dagger tattooed onto it and simply the word 'unity'.

The two lads pulled in a reasonably synchronized fashion, occasionally veering to port then starboard, but overall steered a fairly steady course around the lake. A colony of herons inhabited the island and the family saw two of the majestic birds perched near the waters edge on a fallen tree trunk. Arriving safely back at the jetty they were greeted by a very enthusiastic Major, swishing his tail.

Hand in hand Nick and Tanya strolled along the park paths chatting about the boys, who with the dog, were running between the trees and bushes of the park. Occasionally Major would run back as if to check on the adults, and satisfied that they were still following on, bounded off again to have fun with the youngsters. A miniature railway ran alongside the lake but Tony and Craig considered themselves now to be too old to have a ride.

Reaching the far end of the lake, the family went into the little log style café and sat at the table nearest the window overlooking the one mile stretch of water. A lovely clean little establishment offering quite a varied menu, it enticed them to order some lunch. Major sat faithfully outside feeling a bit leg weary after so much exercise.

It was at this opportune moment that Nick mentioned his late night phone call from Arthur, and the fact that he was having a little reunion that evening. The lads didn't seem to mind at all, but Tanya's facial expression changed somewhat. In a way she was glad for Nick that his mates wanted to keep in touch, but having put up with all those years of uncertainty and of course some of the very boozy nights Nick had enjoyed with the other boot-necks, she just felt a little worried where it might lead.

After their little repast in the café, they walked back to the car. Tanya didn't say very much on the way and Nick felt just a little uneasy about the situation. But then he thought, what the hell, it's only one night, get over it woman, and he began to look forward to seeing his comrades again.

When they got home Tony and Craig went upstairs to play on their computer, Nick put Major in the back garden, made himself and Tanya a cup of tea and the two of them settled on the sofa.

"Are you sure you don't mind?" he asked tentatively.

"No, of course not! Go and enjoy yourself. Just don't get too drunk, remember you are at work tomorrow night," Tanya assured him, with a sting in the tail.

She pulled him to her, they kissed, and he felt such a hug as though a boa constrictor had him around the waist.

"Go on, get yourself ready" she conceded.

Nick went into the bathroom and spruced himself up, ready for his outing. He phoned his usual taxi firm and booked a cab for six thirty. On the dot, the driver peeped his horn and Nick stood in the hallway checking his appearance in the mirror, when the two lads came rushing downstairs to see him off. Nick hugged his sons in turn, his dark brown eyes looking stern but full of love. He shook hands, a long fatherly handshake and said, "You two are the men of the house tonight, so look after your mum for me and I'll see you in the morning. We'll have another great day tomorrow.

Tanya came out of the kitchen along the hallway, wearing an apron and with flour on her hands from baking. On her chin was a smidgen of butter which Nick gently wiped off on his finger, and in turn onto the tea towel on her shoulder. The pair embraced and Nick nuzzled into her neck.

"Are you sure you don't mind?" he asked

"Of course not, go and enjoy yourself, we will be fine."

Tony and Craig felt they were being entrusted with a very important task but knowing that their rock, their dad, would always be there for them. Nick winked his usual reassuring wink to his wife saying,

"Don't worry. See you later." His strong chiselled jaw allowing a smile to crease his cheeks.

The taxi driver peeped again.

He planted a loving kiss on Tanya's forehead and in a time honoured way retracted his right hand inside his jacket sleeve, put the hole next to Tony's nose and said, "Smell that for dead men", gently pushing his fist out to touch his sons nose. A ritual his father had always done to him.

Tony laughed and Craig said, "Better hurry dad, your pint will be getting warm."

Nick opened the front door, turned and asked, "Pick me up later then, around ten thirty?"

Tanya nodded, "No problem, see you later."

The two kissed again and Nick winked at her again. "I've done you a map to the Lion, it's on the front seat of the car."

She scrunched up her face and said, "Get out of here…see you later."

CHAPTER THREE

With some trepidation, Nick entered the White Lion and could hear his buddies laughing. He threw his cap across the room. It land on their table. He strode over to them and the four all shook hands with grips that could crush walnuts. Taff handed Nick his first pint and they all began catching up with each others lives over the last few years.

Arthur was working for the council in Stevenage organising events, setting up meetings and taking charge of charity fundraising evenings. Taff had settled near to Swansea in Neath and was running the local amateur rugby club team, as well as doing some driving for the doctors at his local practice. The Prince had bought a small hotel in Liphook on the edge of the South Downs, with his mother's financial assistance, which his new wife ran with some help from him. He pursued his passion for shooting at the nearby gun club where he spent a lot of his time.

As the evening wore on the inevitable dits arose, each one in turn reminiscing some of the scrapes that they had been in over the years. Largely true, but with the odd embellishment to make it more interesting, more courageous or more funny. Of course there was the obligatory showing of battle scars naming the day, date, time and location of when they occurred.

Interspersing pints with chasers, the bootnecks were thoroughly enjoying their reunion and lost all track of time, when the landlord, Jack, shouted "last orders, gentlemen please."

Nick checked his watch to see it was almost eleven.

Strange he thought that Tanya hadn't arrived yet, but assumed she was allowing him some slack to enjoy time with the lads and ordered another round. The Prince doubled up and the table was quite full with pint pots and chasers to round the night off.

Taff challenged Nick to an arm wrestle, having lost to him on their two previous encounters on a run ashore on Malta. The Prince and Arthur cleared the nearby table and rolling up their sleeves, the two contestants sat opposing each other, and with elbows firmly embedded they gripped hands in a fearsome clench. Locked together, with a fixed stare and in total silence the two combatants took the strain.

Jack, a rather diminutive former Londoner, raced from behind the bar saying "I don't want any trouble here," pushing his glasses up and down on the bridge of his nose.

Arthur put his hand on the little chaps shoulder and assured him that there would be no trouble at all. The tensions between Nick and Taff mounted. Veins began to bulge on both their hands and forearms. Grunting slightly and breathing very shallowly, Taff was determined to exact revenge this time. A side bet of a tenner was wagered quietly between Arthur and the Prince.

Just then the door opened and two uniformed police officers came into the lounge. Nick took his eye off Taff momentarily and the Welshman sent his arm crashing to the table for the first time.

Sergeant Miller, quite a formidable character, stood silently for a moment and scanning the room he asked, "Is there a Clive Nixon in here?"

Taff released his grip.

Nick stood up and squared up to the policeman.

"That's me! What do you want? We were only having a bit of fun."

The sergeant's gaze was almost like a Tussaud statue. Everyone in the pub sat quietly waiting. Sergeant Miller cleared his throat and asked,

"Would you please step outside with me sir, I need to speak with you."

From his tone Nick deduced this was rather more serious than just a bit of arm wrestling fun.

The constable opened the door and the three of them left the lounge. On the car park, Sergeant Miller turned and looking directly at Nick said, "I'm afraid I have some terrible news to tell you."

Nicks eyes, fixed on the bearers pupils, his cold piercing stare almost penetrating the officers skull. Not really wanting to hear the next sentence, Nick demanded "What? What's happened?"

Sergeant Miller said "I'm so very sorry to tell you but there has been an accident on the by-pass involving your family," lowering his eyes to look at the tarmac.

"Not Tanya? No not Tanya! How is she? " his face contorted in anguish.

His pals emerged from the pub and stood behind him. "I'm so very sorry sir, but the accident was very severe and I think you ought to come with us to the hospital straight away."

Nick got into the police car with the two officers and it sped away. Arthur phoned for a taxi.

At the hospital Sgt Miller led Nick to a small office near the reception. "Have a seat, I'll get an update and be back shortly."

Nick felt as though the whole situation wasn't happening and at any moment he would wake up. The constable said, "I'll fetch you some coffee if you like, your eyes look terribly bloodshot."

"You should see them from this side" said Nick.

Sergeant Miller returned moments later and said, "I think you had better sit down."

"Just tell me what's happened." He demanded.

"I'm afraid that your wife and two sons were involved in the collision with a juggernaut about an hour ago on the bypass." The policeman paused, composed himself and continued.

"Your wife I'm afraid suffered critical injuries and died at the scene.

"No! Please god no! Not my beautiful Tanya!"

"Sadly there is more. Your two sons were also in the car and I have to tell you that the youngest, Craig was also pronounced dead at the scene.

"Oh Christ!" Nick stood in disbelief.

"Tony what about Tony he's alright?"

Nick grabbed the sergeants upper arm stripes with his powerful hand grip.

Gently but persuasively, the officer put his hands on Nicks wrists and lowered them to his side.

"Tony is in the operating theatre at the moment, but its touch and go. He has been very badly injured," the sergeant concluded, really devastated having to impart such terrible news, but slightly relieved to have managed to get the words out.

Nick was wringing his hands, almost ripping the very skin off each of them. "They were coming for me. They were picking me up. What the hell happened?"

Nick was really struggling to comprehend what he had just been told.

"It appears that around ten thirty tonight your car was involved in a collision with a eighteen wheeler on the A500. I have no further details at this stage and we are investigating of course.

"How did you know where I was" asked Nick.

"Fortunately that part was relatively easy. Your son Tony had quite a detailed map of a route from your house to the pub in his hand."

"I wrote it down for Tanya. She's pretty hopeless with directions you know."

"Where is Tony? I need to be with him!"

During all his years in service in the marines, in war zones, Nick had encountered some horrific events, but none could compare to the way he felt right now. He was beside himself and completely devastated.

Nick thanked the sergeant for telling him and went past him into the corridor. His former colleagues were standing there, waiting, their facial expressions offering sympathy, but not saying a word having been briefed by the staff nurse of the situation.

Just then the door at the end of the corridor opened and a surgeon dressed in his operating theatre garb, walked slowly towards the group. His face mask was hanging loosely from his neck. The pace was slow almost measured. To Nick everything seemed to be happening in slow motion, black and white. He walked a couple of paces toward the surgeon.

In a very agonised, slow manner, he said "We did everything we could, but… " his voice trailed off.   A spine chilling shriek of "Nooo!" filled the corridor, reverberating off the walls. Nick sank to his knees clutching at the surgeons gown, his head pressed hard into the legs of the man who had just delivered the final blow. He sobbed uncontrollably.

Arthur slowly prized Nick off the medic and lifted him back to his feet. "Come on Nick, let's go back into that office."

The Prince and Taff thanked the surgeon and quietly joined them in the small room. They sat on the plastic chairs.

Total silence prevailed.

Sergeant Miller entered the small room. Nick stood up and looked him in the eyes. "What the hell happened?" he demanded.

The officer said, "It appears that as your wife's car was travelling along the A500 an eighteen wheeler joined the carriageway and collided with it, sending it crashing into the central barrier. The car was sent into a full spin and was then hit again by the lorry and forced back into the barrier. I'm afraid your family stood no chance. The damage was very severe."

"What about the lorry driver?"

"He was OK. We have him in custody at the moment at the station."

"What was he doing? Had he fallen asleep at the wheel or something?" anxiously asked Nick.

"No sir," the sergeant paused. "It appears that he may have been using a hand held mobile phone at the time, but that is all I can say at the moment, until we complete our interview."

"On the phone" For gods sake" Is that it?" Nick's anger boiling he paced around the small office.

His comrades equally devastated not really knowing what to say, if anything. The prince asked the sergeant, "What happens next."

"Well sir, may I suggest that you get your pal home for now, and we'll be in touch tomorrow.

"No! I want to see them. I want to see my wife and boys. I want to see them now!" proclaimed Nick.

"I'm sorry sir, I really don't think that's a good idea right at the moment.

Let the doctors do their work. I'm sure there will be a more appropriate time," Politely insisted the officer, knowing the extent of the injuries.

"Please go home for the moment, and I will come to see you tomorrow."

The three pals agreed and convinced Nick that the best thing to do was leave the hospital, and taking him by the arms they led him outside. He fumbled to open his cigarette packet and scattered several on the ground before finally putting one to his lips. Arthur lit it for him.

Taff phoned for a taxi and after a short wait they all went to Nick's house calling at an off licence on the way for several bottles and cans.

CHAPTER FOUR

Three weeks later Nick opened the curtains and faced yet another dawn. It was a cold, bright morning with clear blue skies. His reflection in the window pane showed up his unkempt appearance, this dishevelled man, denied the usual crisp, smart person he had always been.

Today was going to be the most enduring, gut wrenching, heart crushing time that he'd ever had to face. Determined to do them proud he spruced himself up and stood tall in his grey wedding suit, the only suit he possessed. He had put Major in the back garden, fed and watered. In his inside jacked pocket, Nick put a photo of Tanya and his sons, taken just a couple of months earlier at the barbeque they had enjoyed in the garden, celebrating Tony's twelfth birthday.

The front door bell rang, Nick's comrades stood amid the myriad of floral tributes covering the garden, placed by neighbours, workmates and school friends. Nick opened the front door and retreated to the kitchen, followed by the three men. On the kitchen table was a bottle of Famous Grouse and four crystal whisky glasses. Nick poured very large ones, and in silence the four best friends drank them down in two large gulps.

Tony and Craig's highly polished shoes were side by side on the kitchen floor by the cupboard, just where Nick had put them ready for school that next day. Craig's guitar was leaning against the fridge exactly where he had left it, when he'd helped himself to some cold milk before going with his mum and brother Tony to collect his dad from the pub.

Taff reached down to pick up the guitar and as his hand neared it Nick yelled, "Don't touch that! It's Craig's!"

The Welshman's hand withdrew back to his side like a coiled spring. Apologetically he said, "Sorry Nick, I was only..." his voice petered out in embarrassment.

Quick as a flash Arthur refilled their glasses, raised his hand high in the air and said, "Spirit, courage, determination and unselfishness in the face of adversity!" he downed his drink and slammed the empty glass on the table, swiftly followed by the other three, remembering the Commando spirit and ethos.

"Right, let's do it!" proclaimed Nick.

Just then the front door opened and in walked Aunty Joyce, the last remaining sister of his father. She had travelled by train and taxi from her Manchester home.

The two hugged each other, Aunty Joyce's head only just reaching Nicks chest. Neither Nick nor Tanya had any other relatives. His parents had passed away and Tanya's mum had died in childbirth. She had been brought up in a foster home and adopted by a lovely childless couple who lived in a bungalow at Loggerheads. Sadly they too had left this mortal coil.

"Any chance of a sherry before we go?" asked Joyce.

Nick led her into the kitchen and introduced his mates. Joyce enjoyed a warming glass of Copper Beech.

"That's better," said Joyce, "my whistle was fair parched."

A slight rap on the door from the undertaker heralded the arrival of the funeral cortege.

Outside, lined up were three identical hearses and one funeral car. The bright sunshine glistened on the sapphire black limousines. Four undertakers stood like sentries, one at each car, with the lead man in front of Tanya's, ready to pace down the street. The group left the house and slowly walked past the line up.

On top of Tanya's highly polished mahogany coffin was a single large red rose, while Tony and Craig's each had a small red wreath, their names picked out in white carnations.

As he passed Nick faltered slightly, and gently ran his fingertips along the glass of all three cars, finding it incredulous to believe what was happening, as though he was having an out of body experience.

Surely, this could not be real ?

He joined Arthur, Taff and the Prince, and helped Joyce into the rear of the car. The cortege purred down the road very slowly, travelling about a mile to the village church, arriving just as the clock struck the hour at ten. Most of the village neighbours, all still in shock at the loss of the lovely Nixon family, packed the small building. The local councillors and police officers were there, so too were the two classes from the school Tony and Craig had attended, along with their teachers. Tony's music teacher Mr Brown, and Craig's PE teacher Mr Walley, stood in the small archway entrance to the churchyard.

Several leading members of Nick's 45 Commando Royal Marines formed a line along the pathway, looking resplendent in their uniforms. It was the saddest day to hit the little village of Brampton in its history.

As Tanya's coffin entered the church, Lionel Richie's song, Three times a Lady, played softly in the background, a favourite that Nick had often played for her at home.

Tributes flowed from the vicar and from the school headmaster, their words echoing the thoughts and fond memories of the congregation.

Nick simply stared at the photograph he'd taken from his pocket and in his head could hear their voices. He longed to touch them again, snuggle down with Tanya at his side, and play games with the lads. His faith was being tested to the limit and he just wanted to go and be alone with his thoughts. The sight of those three coffins side by side, would haunt him forever.

Self blame was eating him from the inside, 'If only I hadn't gone to the pub. If only I had booked a taxi home,' he tortured himself with remorseful thoughts. He even began to blame his three oppos for setting up the meeting in the first place, which led to all of this. Mates, through thick and thin for years. His mind was in total turmoil. Unable to think rationally.

When the service ended his fears deepened as he faced the burials. They would prove to be the finality of it all and the realization that Tanya, Tony and Craig were gone, forever. He wanted to die himself but dredged up the courage to carry on for their sakes.

At the graveside, in the shadow of a large, old beech tree, Nick stood resolute as he watched the undertakers lower the three coffins simultaneously, his heart sinking with them. He and Aunty Joyce scattered some earth onto each one as the vicar read the poem, "Do not stand at my grave and weep"

After hugging Joyce and thanking the vicar and undertakers, he turned to his three comrades and shook hands with each one in turn, his steely fixed gaze not allowing any emotion to show.

Then he made a beeline for the Police Superintendent representing the force and heading the case investigation team. He squared up to the uniformed officer, the grip of his handshake almost crushing the bones of his hand and asked,

"When is the court case then? I haven't heard anything from you lot for two weeks."

Slightly taken aback he said, "I'm sorry sir, but all the reports, statements and forensic evidence are all being collated and then we have to wait for the coroner and Crown Prosecution Service. It all takes time to piece everything together." he explained.

"The bastard was on his mobile phone for Gods sake ! What more do you need?" demanded Nick. "My family are in a hole in the ground over there and that cretin is still alive!"

"I know Mr Nixon and I fully understand your anger and frustration, but now is neither the time nor place for this," asserted the officer.

Nick's entire body was wanting to exact revenge on lorry driver Terry Loton, for ploughing into his family car whilst using a mobile phone, and wiping out the last fifteen years of his life and the three most precious people he adored so much.

"Please Mr Nixon, leave it to the courts to settle this," pleaded the super, as he prized his hand free and walked away.

Nick stood silently looking to the ground, his fists clenched so hard that his knuckles were bone white. The funeral party gradually walked away, sensing that he just wanted to be left alone.

They dispersed and left the well kept churchyard, leaving Nick, a solitary figure stooped at the graveside, to privately grieve as a husband and a father.

For the first time that day he felt the tears well up in his eyes as he fondly remembered their perfect wedding day, the births of his two sons, their first days at school, holidays and barbeques complete with burnt sausages. He relived Tony's first win at the 100 metre race and the priceless look on Craig's face when he gave him his first guitar. But mostly, he recalled the day he came home for good from the marines and the sheer joy on all their faces, in anticipation of a wonderful new home life together as a complete family.

He could smell Tanya's perfume, feel her tenderness, see her loving hazel eyes and her warm smile. He stroked his hands together and, eyes closed imagined it was her hand.

At that point the rain began to fall from the clouds that had formed during the service and each drop made gentle plopping sounds as they hit the coffins. Nick stood up and gazed into the heavens, the raindrops mingling with the tears on his cheeks, searching for an answer.

He walked slowly to the waiting car and joined his mates and Aunty Joyce for the short drive back home. The only sound was from the drone of the wipers monotonously beating out a rhythm. Nick had not wanted any fuss afterwards and asked that no arrangements were made for a wake. Instead he had made donations to the church and to the lads school.

The car arrived at Nick's house and the four of them went inside. The Prince poured out the drinks and handed them out, Joyce saying, "I shouldn't really you know, but what the heck, I need warming up after that"

"Before I go, would you do me a favour Clive?" Reaching into her handbag, she produced a mobile phone, a prize she had won recently in a competition, "Show me how to use this, I haven't got a clue with these new gadgets," without really realising the poignancy of mobiles at the time. Willingly, Nick explained how to operate her new link with the world, all the time feeling a little uneasy at the irony of the situation. Her taxi arrived shortly afterwards and she set off back home to Manchester, anxious to get back to her pets.

Drinks flowed and the four friends sat around the lounge talking way into the night. Plots abounded in drink to get the driver on remand, Arthur, Taff and the Prince all had theories on the best way to "take him down", each offering their own skills to do the deed.

Eventually they all drifted off to sleep, their joint snoring would have won prizes for the loudest decibels ever created by just four people.

As usual Nick was awake around six thirty and went for a walk to the newsagents, Major following behind, tail wagging. The early morning mist was beginning to clear. Next door's cat ran across the road and hid beneath a parked car. The local milk float went past rattling bottles in the crates. A flight of starlings swooped across the sky and landed on the ridge tiles of the village pub, their eager eyes scanning around for breakfast.

Nick stood still by the bus stop, lit his first cigarette of the day and thought to himself, 'Life is all still going on as normal, nothing's changed, the world hasn't come to an end'. It all seemed very strange.

As he looked around the village his mind was full of images of his beautiful wife Tanya skipping across the street from the hairdressers towards him, her beaming smile seeking approval for her latest style. Passing the school gates he could see Tony and Craig chatting with their school mates, then running towards their dad on leave, eyes full of expectations for the family weekend ahead.

16

He looked up, drawing deep on his cigarette, and his eyes focussed on the last leaf, hanging by a thread on the might oak tree opposite the post office. Just then it broke free and slowly, gently tumbled down through the branches, twisting and turning as though enjoying its free fall to earth, ending its short life. 'A conclusion is what I need.

The court case.

An end. Loton behind bars.

Only then perhaps, I can have a new beginning,' he thought.

CHAPTER FIVE

Nick placed his newspaper on the hall table and led Major through to the kitchen, opened the back door to the garden for him, while he prepared his dog bowl.

Synchronised snoring could still be heard through the lounge door, as Nick entered and threw back the curtains allowing the sunlight to reveal an array of empty bottles, cans and glasses, surrounding Arthur and Taff crashed out on the armchairs. Begrudgingly the pair woke up, grunting and coughing to the realisation that they had got monumental hangovers.

"Morning lads, fancy a bacon sarnie, and where's the Prince ?" Nick mused.

They both shrugged their shoulders and continued rubbing their eyes.

"What on earth time is it?" asked Taff.

"Seven thirty, you've had a lie in," said nick

"Sadist" replied Taff.

Just then the Prince came bounding downstairs, shaved and showered he beamed, "Hello campers. Who's up for a jog then?"

Taff threw a cushion at him.

An hour or so later, after coffee and toast, Nick thanked them all for their support but politely suggested that he'd really rather be on his own.

"But what about our plans for Loton?" asked the fixer.

"Forget it mate! We can't take the law into our own hands. We've all spent years fighting for justice, let justice prevail in court. He's as guilty as sin, he will get his cumuppence, I'm sure of it." Nick insisted. In the cold, sober light of day, it seemed to make more sense than the fantasy thoughts of revenge plots they had hatched in the early hours, seeing things through the bottom of a bottle. Arthur and Taff said their goodbyes with the strongest of handshakes and the warmest of hugs.

"Let us know the court date Nick, and we'll be there," assured Arthur, as the two left.

"I can stay for a few days if you like Nick? Help you sort things," offered the Prince.

"No, no, you get back home yourself. I really do appreciate everything, but I'd rather be on my own right now." Nick patted Charles on the arm.

After several protestations on both sides, he agreed to go back home to Surrey, insisting that Nick keep him updated with the case developments.

Nick waved him off, closed the front door and surveyed the results of four ex-commandos idea of a good time the night before.

With his military background he set about a big clean up operation. Within a couple of hours he returned the living room to its former pristine state, just as Tanya would have had it. All of the empties in the recycle bin. Everywhere vacuumed and polished. He took special care to polish Tanya's degree photograph hanging proudly above the lads school photographs, which stood either side of one of Nick in his full dress uniform showing his three stripes.

Standing back, he felt justifiably proud of his housework, but then he noticed something missing from the sideboard. The photograph of the four of them together. He pulled open the drawer and as he looked inside he remembered, knocking it off accidentally and 'hiding it'.

Taking it out of the drawer he cut his finger on the broken glass and a few drops seeped through onto the photo, following the crack lines, slowly clouding the image of his face. The clock on the mantel struck the hour of ten causing Nick to jump.

Then silence prevailed, except for the tic toc, tic toc, of the clock which he hadn't really noticed before. It seemed to be getting louder and louder, his brain was working overtime, the anger he felt stirring from deep within wrenched his stomach.

The red mist descended, he began to sweat and the veins at his temples swelled. Nick exploded with fury and threw the photograph he was still holding, at the clock, sending it crashing onto the hearth.

The ticking stopped.

His enraged eyes scanned around the room, empty, silent and lonely. All he could think of was that man on remand, Terry Loton, visualising his bare hands around his throat, strangling the very last gasp from his body. Venting his anger he hurled a brass ornament with some force into the television. The screen imploded with a loud bang, sending shards of glass all over the floor.

Sobbing, he fell to his knees.

Major ran in from the garden barking at the commotion. Seeing his master so upset he nuzzled against him, his bark became a whimper. Nick cupped the dogs face in his hands and vowed, "I will get him. One day I will get him!"

Nick went into the kitchen followed by his faithful companion and washed his hands. He knew that he had a 'chuffer' his term for a spare one or 'one up the chuff', in the kitchen cupboard. Taking the bottle of Grouse he got a large glass and filled it up, added an ice cube and drank it down.

He refilled the glass, lit a cigarette and stood on the back doorstep watching his dog running around the garden chasing his tail.

Staggering slightly he made his way upstairs, crashed out on the bed face down and slept solidly for several hours, not hearing the phone ring nor the doorbell chime. Oblivious in his self induced coma, he relived some of the wartime escapades and scrapes that he and his comrades had endured.

One very vivid memory played out in his mind. They were pinned down in a derelict church in a village in the Garmsir district of southern Helmand province in Afghanistan, after a landmine had exploded under the lead vehicle of their convoy. Six of their fellow marines had been killed outright. Being fired at from two directions by insurgents, the four of them had abandoned their landrover, and made a dash for cover in what was left of this old building.

As the senior officer, Sergeant Clive Nixon, (Nick) quickly assessed their situation, positioning the other three to their best advantage. He sent Corporal Charles Royal (alias the Prince) to the highest point up the remains of some broken steps, with his L96 sniper rifle. This .338 rifle has a range of over one kilometre.

Corporal Arthur Gater (alias The fixer) was positioned behind a large wooden chest near to the entrance, his armoury included three hand grenades. Nick and Corporal Rhys Llewellyn (Taff) took up positions at the back of the room. Taff tried the radio for backup, but it was dead. The dust settled and momentarily all went quiet…, an eerie silence prevailed.

Suddenly the old wooden door burst open and five insurgents rushed in, guns blazing. From his vantage point the Prince fired down, picking off the first three with his deadly accurate aim. From behind the chest Arthur shot the fourth and Taff blasted the last one. Again silence.

Then a blast, an explosion, at the side entrance, sent debris and wooden splinters hurtling into the room in all directions. A piece of wood embedded itself into Nick's right shoulder, the point piercing his skin like an arrow, emerging through his upper back.

Another flying splinter went straight through Arthur's leg, sending him sprawling on the floor in agony, bleeding profusely. Taff was hit by bricks and lay partially covered under the rubble.

Through the chaos and haze of the exploded dust, the Prince, from his vantage point, caught a glimpse of an Afghan, peering in through the front door with his gun raised, ready to pick off any survivors. With his usual deadly accuracy he fired a single rifle shot, taking him out in an instant.

Nick crawled across to Taff and began mauling the bricks off him with his hands, gritting his teeth against the searing pain from his shoulder. Unearthed, he hauled the Welshman up into his arms, wiped the debris from his face and mouth and shouted, "Taff! Taff! Come on mate."

Taff groaned, opened his eyes and in his inimitable welsh brogue asked "what the 'ell 'appened 'ere then?"

The Prince rushed down to Arthur, took off his belt and wrapped it around his leg in a tournakey. He urged Arthur to hold the belt while he ripped off his jacked and then his vest. He wrapped the vest around the wound to stem the bloodflow, and it immediately turned red, but the tight belt quickly began to have an effect and the loss slowed.

Taff got to his feet and ran towards the doorway to assess what was going on outside, knowing that they had to escape and get some medical help pretty damn quick. Seeing just a deserted street, and the remains of the lead vehicle still smouldering a few yards away, he turned back into the room and said, "Come on lads, lets get the 'ell out of 'ere!"

From his position on the ground, Nick raised his gun and fired straight between his legs, hitting another insurgent in the centre of his forehead, stopping him from shooting his 'oppo' in the back.

Two more ran in through the other entrance straight towards Nick. The Prince, out of ammo, threw his dagger hitting the first one in his neck and he fell. The second one grabbed Nick by the throat. Taff raced back and with probably the best rugby tackle he'd ever made, he took the enemy sideways, arm locked his head, twisted and broke his neck.

The Prince picked up Arthur's gun and stood aiming at the entrance. All four knew that their situation was pretty desperate. Nick signalled to the Prince, putting a finger across his lips. He took the grenades from Arthur and passed one to Taff. The pair made their way to the exit and stood either side with their backs to the wall.

With a nod the pair launched the grenades through the gap, hitting the building opposite, taking out the last remaining Afghans of that group. The prince lifted Arthur to his feet. Arthur put his arm around his neck, and hobbled through the doorway.

Nick and Taff opened the doors of their landrover and they all piled in. After several attempts the engine roared into life and with blood running down his back from his shoulder, Nick put his foot down and they sped off.

A loud crack rang out and the side window of the cab shattered. The prince slumped forward and then fell out of the vehicle, hitting the earth and rolling over. Nick hit the brakes and they skidded to a halt. Taff jumped out and returned fire blasting the last remaining insurgent.

In severe pain, Nick ran to the prince, who had been hit in the back, the bullet passed straight through his torso, missing any vital organs. He lifted him up and heaved with all his might to get him back into the landrover.

"How bad is he?" asked Arthur.

"Not sure."

Once again they sped off, towards the medical centre at camp Bastian, Nick feeling weaker and weaker all the way.

Yet again he had relived the nightmare that was Afghanistan.

CHAPTER SIX

After about eight hours 'out of it', he hauled himself off the bed and into the bathroom. He turned on the cold tap and drank copious amounts of water, dousing his face and neck with the staff of life, trying to come around and back to reality. The bathroom mirror beckoned, Nick stared at the broken image looking back at him. Water dripped from his chin. His eyes gradually began to focus, their bloodshot surrounds gave way to the dark piercing pupils that had seen and endured so much.

In his short life he had seen so many of his friends and colleagues blown to bits, shot dead or been so badly injured in this futile war. The nightmares of those dark days and nights would surely haunt him for the rest of his days. But now he had to come to terms with the most personal attack he'd ever had to face. His entire family wiped out by a stranger, driving whilst on the phone, not concentrating.
A single, careless act that totally destroyed his life, taking away Tanya and both his sons in one hit. Now he really had to dig deep. He had to carry on. A task he did not relish.

Nick reached up and turned on the shower, stepped in and stood underneath the soothing downpour for a long time, washing away his past. It did not work. When he stepped out and towelled dry, his thoughts were still very low and revenge filled his mind. He was due back on duty at work at six pm to look after the night shift, having taken several weeks off. How could he face the humdrum of work, his colleagues making platitudes to him, trying to say the right thing, or trying not to say the wrong thing.

Feeling completely clean he dressed in his smart casual clothes and went downstairs. The telephone answer machine was bleeping. His faithful friend Major, was in his basket guarding the wide open kitchen door, his tail wagged a welcome, but he just lay there seemingly aware that his master was troubled. Entering the living room Nick saw the shattered TV screen all over the floor and remembered what he had done. He closed the door, fearful that Major would injure himself on the glass. He patted the dog and said, "bet you're starving old lad, sorry about that mate." He filled the dogs bowl with fresh food and changed the water. Major wolfed the lot and went into the garden.

Nick made himself a large mug of coffee and drank it down, and pressed play on the answerphone.
'Message one received today at twelve o'clock'
"Hello Clive, this is Aunty Joyce, just wanted to check that you're alright."
'Message two received today at two fifteen'
"Hi Nick its Geoff Harrison. Let me know if you are in work today or not, I need to sort cover."

His boss at the security company had initially been quite sympathetic, but was now wanting his pound of flesh.

'Message three, received today at three pm'

"Can you please contact your solicitor, Mr Steve Bladen at your earliest convenience." The voice of Steve's bimbo at Bladen, Bladen, Shawcross and Bladen solicitors.

Feeling hungry himself, Nick did some cheese on toast topped with tomato and mushrooms and another coffee. Major came in from the garden and nudged him as if to say 'I'm ready for my walk now.'

"OK, OK. Just wait a minute, let me sort a few things then we'll go."

He phoned the solicitors first, but their answerphone kicked in, 'we are open between the hours of nine thirty am and five pm, Monday to Friday. I'm sorry, but the office is now closed, please leave a brief message after the tone and we will get back to you as soon as possible'

He rang Aunty Joyce and found her not feeling very well. Advancing years and the onset of the dark, cold winter nights were taking their toll. She had begun to lose weight without any real reason, which in turn led to some anxiety. The anxiety led to a loss of appetite and so the roller coaster was set in motion. Nick promised to go and visit her as soon as he could.

Next he rang his boss. Geoff Harrison answered the phone, "A1 securities."

"Hi Geoff, this is Nick. I really don't feel up to coming in tonight,"

"What? You are putting me in a very awkward situation here. I've got two staff off already, I really need you in tonight!"

"Sorry, I understand but I really don't feel up to it right at this moment. Maybe tomorrow I might feel more like it."

Nick tried to apologise and explain, hoping for just a bit more leeway.

"Come in tonight, or you're sacked" came the reply.

With a sudden rush of blood Nick said "stuff your job where the sun don't shine!"

"That's it, you're fired!" replied Geoff.

Nick put the phone down and knew he probably shouldn't have been so impulsive, but he hated the job anyway and felt that he still needed a bit more time off. Now he had lots of time. He lifted the dogs lead off the hook and said, "Come on then, let's go for that walk."

Major jumped up at him putting his paws on his chest, tail wagging. The pair set off. Walking through the village one or two of the neighbours waved an almost apologetic wave, not knowing whether to speak, or even what to say.

Nick waved back acknowledgingly, not really wanting to get into conversation. When they arrived at the newsagent come off licence, Nick tied the dogs lead to the bin outside and went in to buy cigarettes and a few cans for later.

Unwittingly, he walked straight into a robbery. Three hooded lads were demanding the contents of the till. The shopkeeper, Eric Whalley, a man in his sixties was pinned against the wall by one of the thugs, absolutely terrified but still refusing to open the till.

The other two, brandishing baseball bats were standing menacingly by the cash register. Nick could hardly believe what he was seeing in his relatively quiet village. At the top of his voice he yelled, "Leave him alone!"
The two standing this side of the counter turned on Nick and raced at him with their bats held high. Nick dropped to the floor, swung his legs round and kicked them both to the ground. He reached over and hit the first one an almighty blow to his face.

He rolled over and smashed his elbow into the second lads face. Both were out cold. Leaping to his feet, he bounded over the counter to confront hoodie number three, who immediately let go of the shopkeeper and produced a knife, probably about eight inches long with a serrated edge, he menacingly thrust it towards Nick . For a moment Nick stood perfectly still and simply stared at the lad. His hands at his side, feet slightly spaced, shoulders, head and neck locked in a defiant stance.

The would-be robber waved the knife from side to side, threatening to lunge at any moment. Nick bided his time, mere seconds that seemed to last a long time, and inched his way to the left.
"Come on then!" yelled the lad with an element of fear and panic in his voice.

Calm as a cucumber Nick simply stared at the lad and inched a little more to the left. Eric the shopkeeper, was frozen to the spot, not daring to move for fear of making the situation worse.
One of the two on the floor stirred. Then the lad with the knife thrust it towards Nick. Now in a better position with more room behind the counter, Nick countered the lunging blade with the quickest of hand movements, grabbed his assailant's wrist and twisted, forcing him to drop the weapon. He bent the lads arm, swung him around, placed his other hand behind his head and thrust his face bang onto the counter. Blood streamed from his nose and he yelled out in pain, as Nick forced his arm high up his back.

The hoodie on the floor grabbed his bat and got to his feet determined to help his prostrate mate. As he lifted the bat high to strike a blow towards Nick, the shopkeeper shouted, "No, don't! Stop now. Take the money."

Nick produced his marines dagger (a keepsake that had served him so well in the past, and he had kept on leaving the force, claiming that it had been lost in Afghanistan) and with deadly accuracy propelled it at the lad. The razor sharp blade whistled through the air and cut the lads arm on its way to be embedded in the window frame behind him.

Instinctively he dropped the bat and grabbed his wound with his other hand. "Let's get out of here.!" he yelled and grabbed at his accomplice on the floor. He came round and the pair ran out of the shop leaving the third one still locked in Nick's grip. Nick lifted him up and with his right hand clasped around his throat, banged him up against the wall holding him a good few inches off the ground.

Weary of all this aggro, Nick looked long and hard into the lads eyes and said, "Go away little boy", in quite a soft voice, but conveying a very hard message. He let go and the lad ran out of the shop.

"Are you alright Eric?" he asked

"I am now" he replied, so relieved that it was all over.

Nick retrieved his dagger, concealed it, then standing in front of the counter asked,

"Can I have twenty Bensons and six cans please?"

Still shaking, Eric obliged and refused any payment. Nick nodded and left.

Oblivious to the goings on inside the shop Major waited patiently outside for Nick to emerge. Nick lit a cigarette and untied the dog, and they set off on their walk back home as darkness fell.

Arriving back home he put major into the kitchen and set about clearing up the glass from the living room floor.

That done, he settled on the sofa, pulled a ring pull and sat pondering what on earth he was going to do next. He had no job, virtually no money and no prospects on the horizon. Tanya used to take care of all the household bills with him mostly being away, so he hadn't got a clue about the finances.

The house was rented from a private landlord and most of the furniture and appliances belonged to him too. Nick's only possessions really were their personal effects, nothing of any real monetary value, purely sentimental.

He wasn't even sure whether or not this month's rent had been paid. So on top of everything else the roof over his head may well be in jeopardy.

CHAPTER SEVEN

Brown envelopes began dropping through the letterbox, each containing red demands for all the domestic bills, the worst of which was from his landlord seeking rent arrears. Nick spent several hours searching through drawers full of letters and bills, bank statements and receipts, none of which made the situation any clearer. He knew that he was in a financial mess, the funeral expenses had decimated his bank balance, and apart from his small forces pension had no income at all.

The kitchen cupboards were virtually bare and the fridge contained just a few cans of beer, half a tub of margarine, a couple of sliced of bread and a solitary egg, probably well past it's shelf life. Mindful that he had no way of keeping and feeding Major, he decided he would see if the police force may take him in their training school. With a heavy heart he picked up the phone to arrange it but the line was dead, cut off for non-payment. There was no credit left on his mobile phone either so his only choice was to take the dog to the station and ask in person.

He picked the lead from its hook and his faithful companion Major, wagged his tail in excited anticipation of a walk, not realising that it was to be the last one he would have with Nick. They walked the full six miles to the police station in Hanley, enduring the fine drizzle that persisted all morning. Nick offered the dog to Sergeant Allen from the police dog unit, and he examined Major. He accepted him gladly and asked Nick to sign the necessary paperwork. "What will happen to him?" he asked.
"We'll put him through a series of tests. He will have to cope with loud noise, entering dark buildings, threats from fire and violent behaviour. If he is OK with all that, we'll put him through his paces at our training school, to get him to the required standard. He would then be given to one of our dog handlers and become a vital part of the team. If he were to fail, then we have a list of people keen to have one of our dogs as a pet, we check them out and make periodic visits to ensure they are being well cared for," assured the sergeant.

Nick knelt down in front of Major, cupped his head in his hands and looked regrettably into his big brown eyes. It felt as though he could see his family etched into the dog's memory through those eyes. He patted his bold head, "Good luck fella," he said, stood up and turned away.
Major whimpered. The long walk back home emphasised his loneliness.

Back at the house, Nick set about packing some essential clothes, a couple of bath towels and his shaving gear, into his rucksack. He resigned himself to spending one last night at home before the inevitable repossession would take place. Carefully he put a few photo's of Tanya, Tony and Craig into the side pocket, leaving the empty frames on the sideboard.

He had just four cans of beer left, so he set about drinking them, wondering what to do tomorrow. When he had finished his cans, he took the empties into the kitchen and saw the lads polished shoes and Craig's guitar still in the same position. His heart felt like a lead weight. Again pangs of guilt engulfed his thoughts, self blame brought anger on himself. He felt so lost. He went to bed for the final time in this house, pulled the covers over his head to shut the world out.

In the morning, Nick awoke and knowing he hadn't much time before the inevitable knock on the door, he shaved and showered. He used up the last two rounds of bread for toast and the remaining granules of coffee. Lifting his rucksack onto his shoulder Nick locked up the house and with a very big sigh, closed the door behind him, posted the keys through the letter box, and set off. He had left a note for the landlord, apologising and saying to keep the £650 deposit to cover the outstanding bills.

He called in at the newsagents and bought some cigarettes.

"How are you today Eric?" he asked.

"Not too bad, thanks, but I've put the shop up for sale. I can't bear to be here anymore, the thought of those yobs coming back frightens me. I'm hoping to sell up and go to live down in Torquay near to my sister."

Nick shook his hand and said, "Well good luck and thanks for everything."

"No, Its me who should be thanking you.!" Eric replied. "If ever I can do anything for you, be sure to let me know."

Nick caught the bus into town and went into the Oxfam shop. He gave them the lad's shoes, a bag full of Tanya's clothes and handbags, and Craig's guitar. As he stepped out onto the pavement he felt a little of a sense of closure, but tinged with a profound feeling of loss and sadness.

'Where to go? What to do?' Nick no longer had any purpose or direction.

He walked fairly aimlessly around the town for an hour or so, people watching. After a while he found himself at his old local. Going in, it seemed a bit strange. The pub had recently changed hands so he didn't know the landlord. After several pints and a few chasers he left and walked to the cemetery.

He stood for many a while at the graves of his family, reading over and over the inscriptions on the headstones. As he stood motionless and silent, a robin flew down from the tree and alighted on Tanya's stone. The chirpy little character strutted about for a moment and flew off over the hedge and out of sight.

The early darkness of winter began to fall and as the sun disappeared it became markedly colder. Nick left the cemetery and walked along the lane not really sure where he was going to end up. A gap in the fence led him to the canal towpath and he ambled along reading the names on the narrow boats moored up alongside. When he got to the bridge marked lock 27 he decided that might be a place to get his head down. Out of sight, sheltered from the elements he found a reasonably comfortable position, set a towel on the ground and using his rucksack for a pillow, nodded off into his world of dreams.

A couple of hours later his slumber was shattered by a loud cry and an even louder splash of water right next to him. He awoke and peered through the darkness into the lock. In the water some ten feet down he could see a young man splashing about, momentarily disappearing beneath the surface and re-emerging. Nick scoured the canal side for something to use to reach him. There was nothing.

The lad was too far down to reach and he thought if he jumped in the walls were too steep and slimy to get out again. He called to the lad,
"Don't panic! I'll get you out!"
He raced to the lock gate and by hand, gripping the key like a vice, began to turn the mechanism releasing the water from the higher level into the lock. He could hear the water gushing through the sluice gate gradually getting louder. He turned the key with all his strength to try to speed up the flow.

Nick ran back to the grassy canal side and sure enough the water level was rising, slowly bringing the lad nearer. Removing his belt he wrapped it around one of the mooring posts and holding onto the other end, leaned as far down as he could. He reached down to the stricken lad with his left hand willing the level to rise. The lad was still panicking clutching at the mossy, wet bricks, his fingernails scraping at them, but without anything to grip he kept going under.

Then there was hope, gasping for breath he caught hold of Nick's hand, their fingers interlocked and Nick knew, that he had got him.
He began to pull him out, heaving with all the strength he could muster. His old war wound creased him with pain, his shoulder muscles contracting. His right hand's grip on the belt was slowly slipping. The lad, in abject fear was still thrashing about, not really helping his cause.

Nick dug very deep, tightened his grip on the belt, planted his knees into the soft earth of the grassy towpath, and with one almighty heave he pulled the lad out of the cold murky water onto the pathway.

Saturated, cold and exhausted the lad passed out. Nick set about mouth to mouth resuscitation and chest compressions yelling, "Come on, come on!"
For what seemed like an age Nick battled to revive his rescuee. Limp and lifeless the young boys body lay there, his tender life ebbing away. Nick carried on, (it was not in his character to ever give up), desperately blowing for all his worth, holding the lads nostrils tightly, then changing to chest compressions. Suddenly there was a gurgle, a cough. Nick turned his patient onto his side and the lad began to breath.
"Come on son, you can do it" he pleaded.
A few more coughs and a huge gulp of air and the boy began to move his arms. He opened his eyes and looked at Nick intently.
"Thankyou for getting me out. I thought I wanted to die, but then I got frightened."
Nick took the dry towels from his rucksack and wrapped them around him. He removed his jacket and put it around the lad's shoulders.

28

"What's your name son?" asked Nick.

"Tud, people call me Tud."

"What's your real name?"

"Carl, spelt with a C not a K," he insisted.

"OK Carl with a C, just lie still and I'll get some help."

"Don't leave me!" cried Tud, grabbing Nick's tattooed arm.

"You need to get to hospital, sit tight and I will call for help," Nick reassured him.

"What is UNITY for?"

"Oh that, it's from my days in the marines," he explained.

Nick scrambled up the embankment and climbed over a fence onto the road. Luckily there was a phone box outside a Spar shop about 100 yards away. He sprinted to it, and dialled three nines, gave the location and went back to the bridge overlooking the canal. He scurried back down the towpath. Tud was so pleased to see him.

"An ambulance is on its way. How are you feeling?"

"OK, just a bit cold and a bit sick."

"Don't worry you'll be fine, they'll be here in a minute," said Nick towelling the lad's hair dry.

"What the heck were you doing in the canal anyway?"

"I'd had enough of life in the homes, I can't swim, so I thought that this would be the best way out," said Tud sadly.

"How old are you for goodness sake?"

"Sixteen."

"You have your whole life in front of you!" Nick's frustration made him raise his voice. "Life is precious son, I should know, You must never quit!" he said commandingly and he put his hand on the young lad's shoulder, "Promise me that you will never do anything like that again."

"Ok, I promise mister," Tud muttered quietly, feeling a bit foolish.

"Life is strange with its twists and turns. You will encounter all sorts of different situations and bump into people that may well change your life's path unexpectedly," Nick professed.

"What's your name?"

"Clive, with a C, but people call me Nick."

The sound of approaching police and ambulance sirens filled the air. Nick picked up his rucksack and walked away, not wanting to get involved with the ensuing police enquiries.

"Where are you going Nick?" asked Tud feeling abandoned.

Nick turned, made the shape of a gun with his hand and pretended to fire.

"You'll be fine, sorry I've got to go now."

Blue flashing lights reflected off every surface. Nick wiped his face on his sleeve, lit a cigarette and inhaled deeply. The smoke filled his lungs and somehow relieved the deep feeling of hunger he had. He exhaled and the smoke cloud wafted into the air shrouding his disappearance. The paramedics rapidly arrived and treated the casualty before whisking him off to the hospital.

CHAPTER EIGHT

Two days later Nick was sitting in a café enjoying a cup of coffee, having sneakily plugged his mobile into their socket to recharge when it rang. He answered in his usual manner.

"Hello, Nick."

A young voice asked, "Are you the man who saved my life?"

Nicks body shivered, the nerve ends of his skin made him feel cold. His entire epidermis tingled. He knew the voice of Tud and at the same time wondered how on earth the lad had got his phone number.

"This is Nick, who is that?"

"It's Tud, I just wanted to thank you."

"How did you get my number?"

"You left your jacket. Your notebook was in the pocket. Didn't take me long to decipher your codes. Yours was easy peasy !"

Slightly worried, Nick asked, "So, what do you want?"

"Nothing" replied Tud, feeling a bit rejected, "just wanted to thank you, that's all."

"Fine, no worries kid, have a good life."

Nick pressed the red button and cut the phone conversation dead.

He unplugged his phone, finished his coffee and wandered off along the high street, wondering what he was going to do. Part of him just wanted to disappear and die. But, he had an overwhelming desire to carry on and start again. Not being a quitter, he walked tall and strong entering the park, seeing all the beautiful trees, considering which one to choose for a nights sleep. He found a near perfect place behind a massive old oak tree and set about making a little comfy place to settle.

After about an hour of reasonable slumber he felt the presence of people. He opened his eyes. Aware that he was surrounded, his reaction was to reach for the knife in his sock. Just then he received a massive blow to his head from one of the three, the same lads he had seen off before, attacking the old shopkeeper.

He knew that he was in trouble and swung his legs around, reducing the first one to a heap, then the second assailant hit him so hard with a piece of wood in his chest. Nick grimaced with pain, as the third attacker kicked him in the face. He reeled back his head hitting the ground with a resounding thud. His vision was impaired, but he reached down, pulled the knife out and launched it at the main perpetrator. As the knife penetrated his stomach, he screeched out in agony and fell to the ground. His mates grabbed him up and the three scurried off into the night.

Nick felt sick. The blow to his chest really hurt and the kick to his face had broken his nose and cracked his cheekbone. His vision was still blurred and he lay on the grass motionless, hoping that the pain would go away. He passed out, as the blood streamed from his broken nose, and he became very weak. Nick was in a perilous situation, open to the elements and in a fairly remote part of the park.

A border collie called Lassie, sniffing around in the bushes, out for his usual night stroll with his owner Martin, happened upon this strange object. Lassie began to bark, running around the oak tree and Nick's injured body, bringing his owners attention to this life threatening situation. Martin went to investigate and upon discovering Nick, he immediately phoned the emergency services from his mobile phone.

Nick was taken to the North Staffs University Hospital, where he lay in a coma for two weeks, being fed intravenously. The police had no idea who he was, no way of identifying him as he had no papers or personal possessions to give them a clue, apart from the family photos. His mobile phone had been lost in the undergrowth during the melee by the old oak.

To try to identify this John Doe, the police placed an advert in the local press describing Nick, asking for anyone who knew him to get in touch. In the children's home, Tud took the local evening paper to his room to see what was on TV that night, and saw the appeal. The description matched his hero, Nick, so he raced to the reception and asked if he could use the phone. The master of the homes refused permission and in his usual gruff voice, sent young Tud packing back to his room.

Desperate to contact the police and more importantly his saviour, he escaped through an open window and ran to the village. Finding the old red BT phonebox he rang and the receptionist put him through to Sergeant Miller. "I know that man, the man in the paper, his name is Nick and he saved my life." Sergeant Miller took down the details and asked the lad if he would come to the hospital tomorrow. Tud agreed. He sneaked backed into the home and lay silently in his bed, wondering what had happened to his hero.

The following morning an unmarked police car arrived at the homes and Sergeant Miller asked the matron for Carl to come with him to the hospital. So Carl, or Tud to his mates, went along to identify the man from that dark night in the canal.

Sitting next to Nick in the hospital room, young Tud felt his presence. He felt the strength of this man who had pulled him from the brink that night, when he was determined to end it all in the cold merciless lock.
He gripped Nick's hand with his, and though Nick was wired up to monitors and had a face mask feeding him oxygen, Tud said the same words that Nick had said to him by the canal, "Come on, come on, you can make it."

Nicks grip tightened on the small hand, the reassurance of knowing that someone who cared was there, was priceless. He felt like he had been trampled by a bull. He had a severe headache, his nose was very sore and breathing hurt his ribcage. The youngster went to the water machine and returned with a plastic cup of chilled water. He soaked a tissue from the box on the bedside cabinet and gently wiped his hero's forehead.

Nick slowly opened his eyes and though blurred at first, his vision began to clear and he could see the blonde locks of his visitor. His eyes smiled, the crowsfeet wrinkles said thank you, without words. Encouraged by this reaction, Tud put his right hand into Nick's in a handshake. Nick slowly squeezed an appreciative grip, to say, "I know you are there and are rooting for me." He lapsed back into a deep sleep.

Sergeant Miller quietly asked Tud to come with him to the room opposite, and asked him how he knew the man in the bed. He told him how he had been saved by the mystery person, who gave his name as Clive Nixon, and he used to be in the marines. "OK," the sergeant said, "lets get you back to the home now." "Wait a minute," Tud pleaded, and he nipped back into see nick before he left. Hurriedly he wrote a note and placed it into Nick's open hand, carefully closing his fingers around the piece of paper. He gave him a long, loving stare, touched his cheek and went with the sergeant.

A week later Nick discharged himself from the hospital, thanked the nursing staff and he walked to the nearest pub. He ordered a pint and sat in the corner, then reached into his pocket and took out the crumpled piece of paper. Tud had written, 'Please come and get me. I don't like it here, please help me. I know I can trust you. Tud X.'

Three pints later Nick left the pub and went back to the park, settled beneath the oak tree and slept a deep slumber for the night. He needed to recharge, out in the open, in the fresh air.

Waking at six he felt so much better and ready to start again. His broken ribs were healing and his head and nose were feeling much better. As he collected his meagre belongs together and was leaving, he spotted his mobile phone under a nearby rhododendron bush, so reached down to pick it up, and was amazed to find that it was in one piece and still working. He headed for the local swimming baths and got showered and shaved.

Emerging, he felt the winter sunshine on his face and a clear blue sky heralded a fine day.Checking his wallet he had just forty pounds to his name. He phoned the solicitors to ask if there was any news on the court case. Steve Bladen, his solicitor confirmed the court date was set for November 21st. Nicks anger returned, and the anticipation of that date bore down on him like a ton of bricks. The reality of what had happened, images of his beautiful wife Tanya and his two wonderful sons filled his head, their past, their future, not possible now, all because of this irresponsible driver.

The rage he felt could single-handedly destroy an army.

The solicitor said, "I have written to you advising you of the proceedings, did you not receive my letter?"

Not wanting to reveal his near destitute situation Nick lied, "Oh, probably yes, but I've been visiting relatives so haven't caught up with my post for a while.

Your best bet is to ring my mobile, it's always switched on and always in my pocket.

Nick had three long weeks to wait. Three weeks for his anger to fester and grow to mind blowing proportions, or to try to control it. He reached into his pocket for his cigarettes and out fell the scrap of paper, he had read the day before, scribbled by Tud.

'I don't need these complications' he thought, then read it again. He felt a certain desperation in the note, and tried to imagine if it was one of his sons in that plight. The notepaper was headed 'Penkhull Homes' with the address. Still feeling such pain and anger he walked around the high street, trying to come to terms with everything that had happened. As he walked, he looked into the eyes of people walking towards him. Everyone would surely have a story to tell, everyone would have their own problems to deal with.

He came across a charity shop and in the window a large full length mirror caught his eye, for sale at £10. As he squared up to the window he saw himself as large as life, and stared long and hard at the image in front of him. To the right of the mirror was a small poster inviting donations to help support Penkhull homes, the local children's charity who looked after displaced kids. 'Co-incidence or fate?' Nick decided to visit young Tud.

When he arrived at St Christopher's Avenue he was expecting to see a faceless council type building, having heard of the homes in the past, as a place where only bad kids were sent. The total opposite was true.

It was a beautiful tree lined avenue with large old Victorian houses, very quiet, and almost posh. He approached the first house and knocked at the door, to be greeted by the mother in house 10. She looked after eight youngsters in a home situation, most of her charges being from broken homes and needing a helping hand for a few years.

Nick asked about Carl, she pointed him to home 12 and said to ask for Mr and Mrs Forrester. Walking down the avenue, he thought long and hard what he was going to say to the young lad. He knew that he wanted to see him and thank him for his support at the hospital, but he was inwardly worried what he meant in his note. Standing by the front door, a Brazilian mahogany solid affair, with a bold number 12 screwed to it, he took a deep breath and using the knocker he tapped three loud wraps. The door opened and Mr Forrester stood in the hallway.

The two men eyeballed each other for a moment and Nick reached towards the bearded little man, offering a handshake.

"My name's Nick, I wonder if I might see Carl for a moment, I'm a friend of his."

Len Forrester, a shifty character Nick thought, asked,

"What for? " His gruff voice matched his unwelcoming demeanour.

Nick retorted very assertively, "Because I want to!"

Mr Forrester hissed, "Wait there" and closed the door in his face.

Nick began to see how young Tud could be feeling so unhappy, if he had to put up with this man day after day.

The door opened and Tud's beaming smile as he saw Nick would have melted the toughest heart. He grabbed Nick around the waist sinking the side of his head deep into his stomach.

"I knew you would come, I knew it." He cried with joy.

Cold, hard Nick, felt his hand almost naturally cupping the back of Tud's head reassuringly, stroking his hair.

"What on earth's wrong?" he asked.

"Its horrible here", Tud's eyes wide open appealed to Nick. "The mother is fine, she is lovely and looks after us all very well, but Len, her husband rules this place and is so horrible to us all, and not very nice to his wife either. "Please can you help?"

His big bright blue eyes pleading to his hero with an emptiness, a void, a desperation.

Nick reassured him saying, "Hey don't worry, I'll sort it. Come on, let's go for a walk."

"I can't, I'm not allowed. Mr Forrester would go mad."

Nick banged on the door. Tud cringed and stood back. Len Forrester answered the door.

"I'm taking Carl to the park for a while" Nick said, "is that alright with you?"

His piercing stare and tone of voice meant there could only be one answer. The little bearded man recoiled somewhat, but still wanting to exude power said, "OK, but only an hour and then he has to be back."

Nick put his hand on the mans shoulder, looked deeply into his eyes and tightened his hand onto his clavicle and squeezed so hard that Len's face paled, being more used to dishing out pain than feeling it.

Nick said, "We need a chat, and it will take as long as it takes. OK,"

Belligerent Len meekly asked, "Are you a relative because I have forms to fill in."

Nick stood tall, contempt in his eyes and said, "I'm his uncle. We'll do your stupid forms when we come back, OK."

Tud put his hand into Nick's feeling protected. The pair walked down the avenue to the park, and sat on the swings side by side. Gently rocking too and fro their feet on the ground, they chatted for hours each one getting to know the other better. Tud's parents were killed in a hit and run accident, so he had been in care since. The two bonded in such a superb way, as though fate had destined the situation to be.

"Its time I took you back," conceded Nick.

"Oh no, not back to that place," feared Tud.

"Come on, it can't be that bad surely?"

"I've told you Mrs Forrester is lovely, just like a real mum, but her husband is so horrible, especially to me for some reason. He hates me and always has a go at me. Can't I stay with you?" he pleaded.

Nick, wanting to always be truthful to the lad, said, "I've nowhere for you to stay. See up there, the stars twinkling in the sky? Well, that's my ceiling and down here on the ground, that grass over there, well, that's my bed. You really have to go back and sit it out, well at least for now," he added.

With some reluctance the pair walked back to the homes. Len Forrester was standing in the doorway waiting as Nick and Carl approached. "Eventually you've come back then?" he said somewhat sarcastically. Nick's despise of this person grew. Carl scurried past the master, into the house. The ex-marine reached past Len and pulled the front door closed, took hold of him by his collar and frogmarched him around the side of the house.

Out of sight, Nick said, "When I come back I want to see a very happy, smiling young lad. If I don't, you will be one very sorry man, you sad little person. Understand !"

"If I have to come back any sooner, then you really should start running right now!" For the first time in his life Len Forrester felt real fear.

Nick walked away and heard the front door slam. He turned back and saw Tud's face at the bedroom window, his hand, fingers spread pressed against the glass, more as a sign rather than a wave goodbye. His hero put his hand in the air, palm forwards, mimicking his, then changed it to the shape of a gun and fired an imaginary shot followed by a wink of his eye.

CHAPTER NINE

At last the court date arrived, Thursday the 21st November.
All spruced up Nick set off for the Crown Court and arrived there early. He surveyed the area, taking everything in because he wanted to remember this day. This was to be the day that the villain got his just desserts. He was hoping for a very long prison sentence.

It was a crisp, clear November day. Blue skies betrayed the awful wet summer everyone had endured, as though it was teasing for what might be a harsh winter ahead. He stood solidly on the court steps pondering the outcome and reflected upon what life is really all about. The devastating loss of his entire family had totally transformed his life. From being a dedicated family man with a beautiful loving wife and two wonderful sons to what he had now become. A loner. No real purpose anymore.

Reaching into his pocket he pulled out the now slightly tattered photograph of Tanya and the lads he lovingly carried everywhere. A very large tear began to well up in his right eye, blurring his vision. Not normally an emotional man, far from it, but his whole being was supercharged with adrenalin as he longingly gazed at the photo. Their loving faces, all smiles, took his breath away. Gasping short gulps and swallowing as though his throat was constricted. Nick's heart rate went through the roof, and he could feel his pulse racing. He felt hot, yet a coldness filled his soul and erupted outwards to his very nerve endings sending a shiver around his entire body.

How on earth was he meant to cope with today? Hoping that no one had seen his unmanly display he discreetly wiped away the tear on his cuff and carefully put the photograph back into his jacket pocket. He lit a cigarette, inhaled deeply and told himself, 'Come on, you can do this. You've got to for them!"

It felt that he had built a dam behind his eyelids to hold back the flood of tears welling up. As he walked down the steps to put his cigarette end into the bin a bright reflected flash of light, high up on the rooftop opposite made him look up. There was the outline of a man. Nick peered long and hard against the bright blue sky trying to discern the shape.

For a moment he had a flashback to Iraq. Memories of the Prince high up in the church with his rifle as they were being attacked. 'Can't be?' He thought. Then the man vanished and all he could see was the roofline of the DSS building. He shrugged his shoulders and turned back towards the steps.
'Oh no!' he thought as he walked slowly in the direction of the court entrance, there were several press people, cameras at the ready. The story of the tragedy had hit the headlines when it happened, so only naturally the press had got to follow it up with the court case.

Just then an arm planted itself firmly on his shoulder and a big grinning Welshman hugged Nick like a scrumhalf. "Taff!" Nick could hardly believe that his mate was here.

"Did you think we would let you face this alone boyo? Not likely!" his old comrade said.

"But what on earth is the Prince doing on that roof?" Nick demanded.

"Never you mind about him, he'll be alright" reassured Taff.

As they were speaking Nick's solicitor arrived. He appeared to have come straight out of the trouser press, not a pinstripe out of place. His firm handshake and confident air bolstered Nick's mindset towards the forthcoming proceedings.

"Excuse us," he said politely to Taff leading Nick up the steps, "we have a few matters to discuss before going into court."

Entering a small anti room the solicitor suggested that Nick had a seat, his previous confident, almost flamboyant attitude, took on a more cautious tone. Nick's heart began to feel heavy. Steve, his straight talking solicitor took the seat opposite and after a slight pause, he said,

"Originally I was certain that we had a watertight case, but I've had some news just this morning that the defence are to challenge a vital piece of the police evidence, and one particular aspect of their procedure immediately after the crash."

"What ?" gasped Nick. "At this late stage" I thought we had him banged to rights!"

"I know, I know," said Steve, "but unfortunately nothing is ever certain."

"You mean he could get off?" Nick was on his feet with total disbelief etched across his face.

"You told me that he should be facing seven to ten years for what he did!" Nick's anger now taking on a new dimension.

"I will do all that I can, you know that, but in the light of this new technicality, he may well be facing a much lesser sentence, if indeed a sentence at all, bearing in mind he has spent three months in custody so far," explained Steve very reluctantly.

Pacing the small room Nick found this bombshell absolutely incredible. How could this be happening. Was there no justice anymore?

"I need a cigarette," he said curtly, as he pushed past his solicitor and out of the office.

Standing a the top step he searched for Taff, and spotting him on the corner of the street, bounded down the flight of ten steps in just three jumps. Grabbing the Welshman's arms Nick questioned his intentions.

"What's your plan, why is Charlie on the roof?"

"Calm down, calm down, what's the matter then?"

Taff knew that look and tried to take the sting out of the situation.

"My brief says he might get off that's what's wrong. After all this, he could walk free!" Nick hardly believing the words he was saying himself.

"We, that is me, the Prince and Arthur thought that in the event of him getting away with it, we would take him down for you. Swift, clean and no comebacks. You would be with your solid alibi, your solicitor. No-one would ever know, so that's what we've planned. If he gets sent down then we would just stand down," clarified Taff.

"Do it for me. Do it for Tanya and the lads. I don't want him to breathe for one more day!" Nick's frustration spilling over to his friend.

The pair shook hands looking each other eye to eye and Nick ran back up the court steps. Taff took out a walkie talkie handset, pressed the button and said, "It's on! The mark must go today!" Both Arthur and Charlie received the brief message.

Nick took his seat in No1 Court alongside his solicitor. The room felt cold and totally without any feeling, a monument to the British legal system. Almost sterile. The defendant's lawyer arrived and began to set out their papers on the polished oak desks in front of them. Nick sat in silence wrenching his hands together, not believing what seemed to be happening all around him.

Outside, a white, unlettered van was parked in the small side street next to the court, on double yellow lines, engine running. Bearded Arthur was sat behind the wheel patiently waiting. The press men were now gathered at the top of the ramp leading down and behind the old Victorian building hoping to snatch a photograph of the accused.

A police patrol car preceded the prison van bringing the prisoner to court. The two vehicles approached and suddenly there was a screech of tyres as the white van accelerated forwards and stopped, blocking their way. They came to a sudden stop. The barrel of the Prince's rifle appeared over the parapet opposite and an almighty loud crack made everyone in the vicinity jump. Glass shattered into the prison van as the bullet hit, sounding like a small explosion. Trained on the opening Charlie's eye could see two heads through the sight. Decision made, he squeezed the trigger for the second time, the loud crack breaking the eerie silence engulfing the square.

The second projectile entering the open van window with electrifying speed, just as the van driver lurched the vehicle forward, bumping into the back of the police car. Arthur's van sped off and disappeared round the corner. The police car and the security van raced down the ramp and behind the building.

Picking themselves up off the ground the men from the daily's hurriedly took flash photos of the van with the smashed window, as it raced past them. Within minutes the wailing of police sirens filled the air as dozens of blues and two's raced to the scene. An ambulance raced down the ramp parking next to the prison van. Two paramedics jumped out and climbed inside carrying their first aid gear.

A police helicopter hovered above, turning slowly 360 degrees the camera operator searching for the white van, described only as a transit sized white unlettered van, bearing German number plates.

Inside the courtroom they were oblivious to the commotion ensuing beyond the walls, until a clerk entered and advised everyone that all proceedings had been suspended and that they should all go to the waiting room and await further instructions.

Nick could feel sweat beads running down his back, not really knowing, but having a shrewd idea, that his comrades had struck. He went with his solicitor to the small office in which they had spoken earlier.

"What the heck's going on?" he asked.

"I really don't know, but obviously something has happened to cause a delay. Sit tight and I will try to find out," Steve said.

In the foyer people were scurrying about. The sirens had now stopped but looking outside Steve could see several police cars, and uniformed officers taking instructions from a police superintendent at the foot of the steps. He questioned the court official who simply said that somebody had been shot.

Arthur 'the fixer', had rounded the corner after the second shot, picked up Taff and raced down the next street where the Prince, having descended from the roof, stood beside an open door to a lock up garage. Arthur drove straight in and switched off the engine. He and Taff came out and climbed into a Vectra parked on the pavement, the Prince closed the lock-up and jumped into the car. Arthur put his foot down and they were away.

The police helicopter continued hovering around the surrounding area and police cars were racing up and down the town's streets searching for this white van from Deutschland, but all to no avail.

Twenty minutes later and the three ex soldiers were sixteen miles away at Crewe railway station. Taff boarded a train to South Wales and Arthur and the Prince drove south to Worcester.

They parked on a supermarket car park and walked to the other side, calmly getting into a Volvo Arthur had left there earlier. The two drove off. Mission accomplished, or so they thought.

Nick could not contain himself any longer and left the office in search of his solicitor. He spotted Steve in deep discussion with other suited and booted types. He approached the group just as they began to disperse.

"So what's going on then for pity's sake?" he said agitatedly to Steve.

"It seems that a shot has been fired at the defendant and he is being treated at the back of the building," explained Steve.

"A shot, what do you mean a shot? Is he dead?"

said Nick, putting on a false concern to his voice.

"No, no. It's just superficial apparently. Stay here I'll try to get some more information," he replied.

Nicks anticipation of his comrade's actions seemed somewhat unfounded suddenly. His mind was doing 100 miles an hour yet again.

He went towards the exit to have a cigarette outside but his path was blocked by a rather burly court official.

"Sorry sir, no-one is to leave the building."

Nicks frustration surfaced. "I'm not leaving, I just need a cigarette outside," he said angrily, pushing the man to one side he opened the door, stepped out and lit a cigarette.

A police sergeant put a hand on the door official's shoulder knowing who Nick was and what he was facing. "Just leave it," he said, and stepped outside to join Nick.

"Can I get you anything Mr Nixon, a coffee perhaps?" he enquired.

"No, you're alright, but thankyou, I just need to know what's happening."

"We are waiting on the judge to decide if the case will open today or be postponed in the light of what's happened. We will let you know just as soon as we know. Now, please come back inside. I appreciate how difficult it must be for you, but I assure you that we all want a conclusion as soon as possible."

The sergeant opened the door and motioned him back inside.

Nick obliged and stepped back in.

His solicitor came over and said, "The judge wants to open and adjourn the case today. We need to go into the courtroom right away."

Judge Fraser Mortimer called the two solicitors to approach the bench. He issued his directions and the two returned to their places.

Two security guards appeared flanking the defendant and took their place in the dock. In all of his thirty seven years on this planet Nick thought he had experienced every emotion possible, but seeing Terry Loton… for the first time face to face, in the same room, he felt a hatred so deep, so totally all consuming it transcended every single previous experience.

Nick's gaze was transfixed on the man standing in the dock. He had his left ear covered with a dressing and there was dried blood on his collar. He was asked to confirm his name and address. The clerk of the court asked, "Is your name Klaus Vilner?"

The defendant responded simply, "Yes."

Nick could not believe his ears. He leapt to his feet exclaiming, "Liar! You're Terry Loton!"

"Silence in the court," boomed the judge.

Steve pulled Nick back to his seat. The clerk asked the defendant to confirm his home address in Leeds.

"That's correct," he said.

"You are charged that on the 2nd of August 2008 you caused death by careless driving, do you understand the charge against you?" asked the clerk.

"Yes sir," he answered.

"To that charge how do you plead, guilty or not guilty?"

"Not guilty" he replied

"There has been no application for bail ma' Lord," the clerk informed the judge.

The judge declared the case open and adjourned it to reconvene in six days time, on Wednesday the 27th November, at ten o'clock, to give the defendant time to recover from his injury.

"All rise," demanded the clerk, and the judge retired to his chambers.

The guards took the defendant back down the stairs.

In total disbelief Nick rounded on Steve.

"Who the hell is Klaus Vilner?" And what's happened to the charge? It was dangerous driving, not careless!"

"Let's go to my room and I'll explain what's happened," Steve said as he gathered his papers together. Once in the office the solicitor began to explain that new evidence had come to light in the last twenty four hours.

He said that he had only been informed moments before the trial was to start that Terry Loton's real name was in fact Klaus Vilner, he had changed it seven years ago to protect his identity. His elder brother Wilhelm Vilner had been part of a radical cell at a university in Germany and had links with a terrorist group. In 2001 Klaus testified against his brother who was subsequently jailed for ten years for his part in a failed terrorist assassination attempt in The Hague. Fearing reprisals he changed his identity and was allowed to settle here in Leeds for his co-operation, with the help of the then Home Secretary and the Ministry of Defence.

Nick was shaking his head, pacing the small room trying to understand how all of this had only now come to light.

"Unfortunately there's more," some trepidation in Steve's voice. "I think maybe you should sit down."

Nick spun around and glared at him. "More what?"

"The police video tape of the accident showing Vilner on his mobile phone from the overhead gantry has disappeared, that's why the charge has been reduced from dangerous to careless driving. Without that tape we have no proof that he was on the phone at the time of the crash," said Steve, knowing what a crushing blow that was to Nick.

"I don't believe this is happening" Where's the watertight case? We've got nothing!" In anger Nick thumped the door.

"What about the mobile phone record then?" he implored, "surely they can prove it?"

"Sadly that record was with the tape that disappeared," sighed Steve, raising his eyebrows but not Nick's hopes.

A loud knock at the door gave them both a start.

Police Sgt. Chetwynd came in, accompanied by two uniformed officers.

"Mr Nixon I'm afraid I need to ask you some questions about the shooting."

"Ask me some questions? What for?" replied Nick.

"You were seen outside the court building talking to a man earlier, who was he?" asked the sergeant.

"Oh him, just a chap I met in a pub the other day wishing me luck with the case," dismissed Nick.

"You wouldn't happen to know his name would you?"

"Erm.. Bill, that's it Bill."

Nick was now nervous about his comrades and what had happened to them.

"Bill what sir. What's Bills surname?" he probed.

"I don't think he ever said," said Nick.

"Which pub was it you met in then?"

"Oh I'm not sure, could have been the Albion or was it the Eagle? Really I don't remember."

Steve butted in at this point, "Sergeant, can I ask where these questions are leading? You cannot surely be linking my client with the shooting incident! He was in court with me when it happened."

"Yes we know that sir, but we have to investigate the matter, and with Mr Nixon's past military experience we have got to consider all angles at this stage."

"Well may I suggest that you leave your questions for another less stressful time than this and leave my client in peace," he firmly told the officer.

"Very well sir, for now we'll leave it, but we will be making enquiries at the two pubs you mentioned and no doubt will be talking with you again." At that the police left.

Nick looked at Steve and said, "I need a drink, I'm going. I will see you tomorrow!"

He felt that he couldn't say anymore until he knew that his pals were OK and he left the court.

Mindful that he may be followed Nick caught a bus and travelled to the next town. Alighting from the bus he crossed the busy street and walked a few hundred yards to the taxi rank. He got into the front taxi in the queue and asked to be taken to Newcastle, a distance of about five miles. Halfway there he told the cab driver that he had just remembered something and could he go instead to Burslem. Obligingly the driver doubled back about a mile and then went onto the 'mother town' of the Potteries.

Nick walked along the high street and down an alleyway known locally as Cocks Yard. Satisfied that he wasn't being followed, he went to a public phone box and rang the Prince on his mobile. They kept the chat very brief and set up a meeting for seven pm at the motorway services at Keele. The meeting was most enlightening.

The Prince explained to Nick how his mother had entertained a QC and his wife earlier in the week and after several drinks the old Etonian friend of hers allowed the brandy to loosen his tongue. He let slip that one of his colleagues was working on a very interesting case "up north" in Stoke on Trent. Knowing the tragic events that happened to Nick, Charles's friend, and that he was from that area, she posed a few probing questions.

The babbling QC told her, in complete confidence of course, that the accused was subject to special treatment for his not inconsiderable role in the trial in The Hague Bomber Plot and all these unfortunate events were to be swept away for the sake of diplomacy. Some of the top echelons of power in the secret service had been involved.

Wanting to further her own business she often entertained the so-called upper class and her cosy dinner parties were gaining a good reputation. She happily plied him with brandy in exchange for all this inside information knowing that Nick was such a very close friend of her son Charles, and how terribly sad she had felt when she heard the news of his families tragic deaths.

In fact she had met Tanya, Tony and Craig just once, probably two years earlier, on a visit to the Potteries with her son when she was on a mission to buy Wedgwood Pottery to enhance her stock in the shop. She remembered Tanya's beaming smile, the sincerity she exuded and how polite the two lads were. So, she quite happily, without conscience passed on what he had said, in confidence of course.

The Prince apologised for his shot missing. The problem was he explained, once the van window was smashed he could see two people sitting on the bench in the back who looked similar. He logically thought the chances are that the guard would have his left hand cuffed to the prisoner's right and so chose the guy on the right to aim at. He had the centre of his forehead in his sight and pulled the trigger just as the van lurched forward. His bullet caught Vilner's left ear. There was not time for another shot as the van turned to the right and down the ramp.

Nick said, "Hey, no worries, thanks for having a go, but I'm worried about Taff, he was seen talking to me outside the court before the shot."

The Prince smiled reassuringly, "He was in Swansea all day at a wedding surrounded by at least fifty witnesses."

"What about Arthur?" asked Nick.

"Again no worries, it's all sorted, he was pot holing in Derbyshire with three solid mates."

"What about you?"

"Escorting dear mama on a shopping trip to Chester my good man…

The van we used as a blocker was German registered, the rifle was German and so were the cartridges. Plod will find them in a lock up nearby, so too the shell cases on the roof. They will assume it to be a revenge attack connected to his brother who's incarcerated courtesy of Klaus" he explained.

Nick said, "I can't believe that you've all gone to so much trouble for me."

"We haven't just done it for you Nick, we've done it for Tanya and the boys too you know!"

"I know, it's really appreciated, but it sounds like this one's got us beaten. He's likely to walk away on Wednesday."

"Not bloody likely! We'll get him next time" the Prince exclaimed.

"No!" pronounced Nick, "No more! I couldn't bear to see any of you three get into trouble. Let it end here and now. Thanks for everything but I'll deal with it myself," he dismissed his pal.

Their firm handshake sealed it.

Nick walked away, and turning back, he waved at the Prince and said, "He's mine!"

CHAPTER TEN

Nick left the service station and headed back to the village. He had taken a short term let of the flat above the off licence from his friend Eric, who lived downstairs at the back of the shop. There was no charge for the accommodation as Eric was just pleased to help, and the peace of mind that someone else was there was priceless. He lived in fear of being robbed again and had put the business up for sale after spending the majority of his life building it up.

Avoiding conversation Nick entered the flat through the side door and closed it behind him quietly. At the top of the stairs he went into the living room and shut the door. The room, although a brief sanctuary, felt as empty as he did inside right now. It had been a harrowing day with climaxes and anti-climaxes. He had expected to see Loton (or Vilner) sent down for what he had done. Then he had hoped his army buddies would have dispatched him.

What to do next, that was the problem. He'd got the whole of the weekend to ponder how to deal with the situation and the dread of Wednesday looming large in his mind. He couldn't get Vilners' face out of his head.
That smug look purveying an almost untouchable arrogance. Obviously he had never come across Clive Nixon before. His resolve was steadfast, but how on earth could he wreak revenge?

Pouring a large scotch he sat at his little breakfast bar, sipping and searching every corner of the grey cells trying to work it all out. From what his solicitor had told him about the tape evidence and the mobile phone records being lost, or, as he put it, 'disappeared', and without any first hand witness the case seemed doomed to failure.

The thought of that man walking free to carry on his life as though nothing had happened didn't bear contemplating. He was obviously a nasty piece of work to have testified against his very own brother. But then Nick considered that for while… Was he really that bad? He had helped put a terrorist behind bars. Could that be a bad thing, even though it was his very own brother? But what was his involvement, and what charges might he have faced if he had not co-operated?

A second glass of Famous Grouse did not make any more sense of things either, but it went down well. Very tired, Nick decided to turn in and sleep on it till tomorrow. Perhaps he would have a better, clearer take on things in the morning. And he had to go to the solicitors again.

As usual he plugged his mobile phone in to charge up overnight and placed it on his bedside cabinet. There was a message he'd missed.
It was from Aunty Joyce asking how the case had gone, apologising for not attending, but still feeling poorly. Oh damn! He thought, I promised to ring and let her know. The alarm clock showed 10.50pm. Too late now he thought, better to ring her in the morning. He switched off the light and drifted off.

He had the most restless night, tossing and turning, so many thoughts in his head. Part of the night was reliving happy times with Tanya and his two lads. Precious moments. She had been such a wonderful mother, spending so much time helping with their development, mostly single-handedly, while he was away on duty. He regretted missing some of their childhood. Part of the night his thoughts were of his three best mates. All individual characters but all the same when it came to their friendship. They shared a very close bond, almost like family.

Then his thoughts were back with Vilner. He visualised choking the last breath from his body with his bare hands throttling his neck. Shaking his head violently and staring deep into his eyes, penetrating his mind. With a jolt Nick awoke. He was sopping wet. Beads of sweat on his forehead combining and running down his face. Realising it was only a dream he washed and slumped back into bed. The clock showed 4.30am so he thought he'd got a few hours, and after a while he managed to slip back to sleep.

What seemed like just moments later, Nick awoke. It was 7.20am . He had by his standards had a lie in. Shaved and showered he quickly dressed and had his usual mug of tea and cigarette standing on the back doorstep. It was another cold, grey day.

He rang Aunty Joyce at 8am. A strange female voice answered the phone. Nick asked who it was. "Nurse Bourne here, who are you?"

"Nick! What's happened to Aunty Joyce?"

"She's sleeping at the moment, are you a relative?"

"Yes, I'm, Nick her nephew, how is she?"

"Not too good I'm afraid, she's had a peaceful night, the doctor is due here shortly. Would you like me to ring you back when he's been?"

"No! I'm on my way right now!

Nick grabbed a few things together and raced to the railway station. Hurriedly he bought a ticket and stood on platform two impatiently waiting for the train. Several commuters stood nearby, some looking a bit bleary eyed from the night before and others on mobile phones chatting away with the volume of their voices allowing anyone within fifty yards to share their one way conversation without really wanting to.

His thoughts were with Aunty Joyce. She had been such a rock throughout his life and he was on a bit of a guilt trip because in recent years he hadn't kept in touch as much as he should have.

The train arrived, only ten minutes late and Nick boarded taking a window seat. Moments later the train shuddered into motion and set off north. Nick settled back thinking that he had got an hour to compose his thoughts and think of some nice things to say to his beloved aunt.

Just then a 'cowboy' got on and took the seat opposite Nick. The man was wearing a Stetson hat, his long hair way below his shoulders mingled with his full beard, which must have taken years to grow. He was wearing a proper cowboy style waistcoat and a shoelace necktie. At his sides he had two leather pouches suspended from a leather thong around his neck. But, the most striking feature of this strange man was that he was totally bare foot, and his toenails were painted blue.

He looked across the table at Nick and through the friendliest of smiles said, "Hello".

They engaged in conversation and Nick discovered that the odd looking character was called Pete the feet, given that name because he walked everywhere barefoot, regardless of the season or temperature. Hailing from Moseley in the West Midlands Pete often travelled by train and if he liked the look of a place when the train stopped at a station, he would get off and have a look round.

Moseley, a suburb of Britain's second city, mentioned in the Domesday Book, had been home to Pete for some years and he was very well known there. He regarded Birmingham as his out of town shopping centre. The reason for his unusual behaviour was that he quite simply could not stand to wear shoes and socks as they made his feet smell. He felt so much more comfortable barefoot and the reason he painted his toenails was to conceal the dust that attracted itself under his toenails making them appear dirty, whereas in reality he washed his feet more often than most.

"People used to say the reason I took my shoes and socks off was as a protest against the Vietnam war, and I would only put them back on again when the war was over. It was a load of rubbish. I did it because it felt comfortable. As long as I was comfortable with myself, then that was OK, nothing else mattered."

Nick was totally fascinated by Pete's story and the two had a thoroughly interesting chat as the train sped along the track. Pete explained that the Stetson was the most practical of hats. "Keeps the rain off, keeps the sun off, keeps the cold out, keeps the heat in." His hobby was making cigarette lighter covers out of leather. Individually hand stitched cases in an array of colours and styles, but each on had its own unique Pete the feet emblem of two tiny bare feet imprinted on them.

He produced a selection from the pouches at his side and laid them out on the table in front of Nick and invited him to choose one.

"How much are they?" enquired Nick.

"There's no charge at all. Have one. My reward is simply to put a smile on someone's face."

Nick chose a tan coloured case, hand stitched with the feet emblem on the back and a lions head on the front, and smiled. The pair disembarked at Manchester and parted company. Nick felt that his life had been enriched by meeting the affable cowboy from Moseley.

Nick hailed a taxi and sped off to Aunty Joyce's. The light relief he had just enjoyed paled as the black cab approached her street. The driver turned the corner and Nick looked past his head, to see an ambulance parked outside her house. Paying the fare quickly he raced along the pavement, through her front gate, and up the path to the front door. He was met at the doorway by Doctor Tommey. His expression said it all. "Sorry, there was nothing I could do, sorry!

His heart sank, yet again, and he walked inside the house to see the paramedics collecting their equipment together. They stepped aside to allow Nick access to see Joyce 'fast asleep' on the bed in the bedroom of her bungalow. Tears welled up in his eyes and he sat next to her taking her hand in his. He gently pushed her fringe back off her forehead, leant forward and planted a loving farewell kiss on her peach like skin.

After a few moments of silence he left the bedroom and went into the living room. The old grandfather clock tick tocking away in the corner marking out the seconds of life. He poured himself a sherry from the crystal glass decanter on the sideboard, her favourite tipple.

"Cheers Aunty Joyce. Sorry I wasn't here ," he said quietly
The medic came in and asked if he was OK. Nick simply nodded.
"The undertaker will arrive shortly, we have to go. Will you be alright? Would you like me to call a relative for you?"
"No. I'll be fine thanks. I'll sort everything," he sighed.

The medics left and Nick poured himself another sherry. Lots of memories flooded back as he looked around the living room filled with Aunty Joyce's possessions and photographs. She had an array of framed snaps set out on an antique, highly polished sideboard, all sitting neatly on a hand crocheted white linen tablecloth, mostly of Tanya and the boys and a few of Major.

The doctor had left his handwritten note on the coffee table, certifying his aunt's death. Nick read it through and put it into his pocket knowing he would have to go and get it registered.

When the undertakers had been and gone Nick checked that all the windows and doors were secure. On his way out he noticed the mobile phone on the hall table, picked it up and popped it into his pocket.

As he was leaving he was greeted at the front door by Mr Armstrong a neighbour, who he had met a couple of times.
"I'm sorry to hear about your Aunt," he said.
The pair shook hands. "Thanks!"
"Is there anything I can do?"
"No. Thankyou anyway, but there's not much any of us can do at the moment.
Nick closed the door and began to walk down the path, followed by the neighbour. As they got to the gate Mr Armstrong said,
"I know this is probably not the right time but..."
"But what ?"
"If you decide to put the bungalow on the market would you please give me the first option to buy it. My daughter lives down south and is desperate to come and live nearer to us." He gave Nick his phone number on a piece of paper.
"I'll bear it in mind," replied Nick.

He decided to walk to the railway station to clear his head. It was quite a long walk but it gave him some time to gather his thoughts together.

CHAPTER ELEVEN

Arriving back at Stoke station at around 2pm he remembered that he was supposed to have seen his solicitor earlier, so he hurried along to his offices. He entered the somewhat sombre building and into the small reception area. The décor dated back to the seventies and the furniture even earlier. Nick pressed the enquiries bell to the left of the little frosted glass hatch. One of the glass panels slid open and the receptionist, a middle aged spinster, looked over her half moon reading glasses and simply said, "Yes?"

"I need to see, Steve."

"Sorry he's out."

"Out?"

"Yes, he's been called away on an important case and won't be back today," she said.

Nick was not too disappointed, he felt that he'd had enough for one day and really hadn't relished the thought of going through all the legal arguments of the court case, even though thoughts of Vilner were paramount on his mind. "Will he be in tomorrow?"

"No, it's the weekend, we do not open at the weekend," she pointed out.

"My court case is on Wednesday, I really ought to see him before then," he explained.

The receptionist turned and got the diary. Opening the page for Monday she said, "He has an appointment with a client at 10am."

"Could I see him before that?"

"I can pencil you in for nine fifteen but I can't guarantee that he will see you," she said.

"Fine, I'll be here. Thankyou."

She closed the frosted glass pane.

Nick left the office and walked around for a while rather aimlessly, when he came across an old haunt, a quaint little pub called the Prince Albert. Fancying a pint he went in and was pleasantly surprised to recognise a familiar face from those days, Barbara the barmaid, still behind the bar.

"Good heavens above!" she exclaimed, "Never expected to see you again!"

"You know me, just like a bad penny. Pour me a pint please Babs and have one yourself," he smiled.

Barbara, a rather attractive brunette with the customary low cut blouse to attract the punters, obliged and presented Nick with a cool clear pint topped with a good head.

He took it up and drank it down in just three or four gulps, wiped the froth from his top lip, and put the glass on the bar.

"Same again please," he said.

"So what brings you to this neck of the woods then Nick and where have you been?"

"Oh, just passing by and thought that I would pop in for a quick one for old times sake. I didn't expect to see you still here though. I thought you were going off to live in Spain with, er, what's his name?"

"You mean Phil? Yeah, that was the plan but he forgot to mention that he had a wife and three kids, the rat."

"Sorry, didn't mean to open old wounds," he apologised and took a sip from his second pint.

"So who's the love of your life now then Babs?"

"Myself, that's who. I've totally given up on men. I've had my fill of being hurt so it's just me and Jasper now, thankyou very much," she said in a resigned way, but still with a cheeky sparkle in her eyes and a broad smile that dimpled her cheeks enticingly.

"Jasper?" enquired Nick.

"The moggy over there," Barbara pointed to a rather overweight feline on the chair in the corner, curled up fast asleep.

"So where have you been hiding yourself then Nick all these years?"

"Here and there you know. I had a spell in Iraq and then two tours in Afghanistan, but I'm back here now, well at least for the moment, who knows what tomorrow will bring?" he explained, trying to keep the conversation at arms length.

He finished his pint and put the glass down on the bar, thinking to leave, but Barbara said, "Have this one on me then, for old time's sake before you go," and refilled his glass.

"Cheers!" said Nick gratefully and moved over to the bandit to try a few quid. He lost at first, then with his next attempt dropped the forty pound jackpot. Barbara came out from behind the bar to collect some glasses. "Well done!" as she patted him on the back and noticed he had a button missing from his jacket, "Hey scruff, where's your button?"

"It's here in my pocket, it came off in my hand."

"Take it off and give it to me, I'll sew it back on for you."

"No, honestly, it's alright, I'll do it."

"Nonsense. Do as you're told! Give it here," she insisted

Nick removed his jacket and handed it to her with the wayward button.

While she was in the living quarters, Nick bought another pint and a double whisky chaser from the part-time barman and sat on the stool at the end of the bar. The noise of the juke box and all the customer's voices, increasingly louder and louder to combat the music, began to grate on his nerves.

Barbara emerged, her handiwork complete.

"There you go soldier, good as new!"

"Thanks. I was going to do it myself but…."his sentence petered out and he stared a thousand yard stare towards the floor in deep contemplation.

Thinking back, to when Tanya used to do all the mending at home.

Barbara sat on the adjacent stool and signalled to Mike the barman, to refill hers and Nick's glasses.

"So how's the family then Nick?" she asked.

The question pierced his brain like needles. He tensed up unable to face up to the reality of what had happened. A cold sweat engulfed him and the room began to spin. His eyes glazed over and he fell from the stool crashing to the floor in a heap. A combination of very little sleep, no food and drinking causing a temporary shut down.

Barbara, a former nurse, checked his pulse.

"Give me a hand here," she demanded. Two of the regulars and Mike, lifted Nick up and carried him through to the living room, laying him on the sofa. Barbara had soaked a bar towel under the cold tap behind the bar and she placed it over his forehead. She removed his shoes and covered him with a blanket. Jasper the cat, wandered through from the bar not showing much interest in the goings on, and stepped outside through the cat-flap to pursue his nocturnal roaming.

Nick began to snore for England so Barbara closed the door to the living room and went back to serving. When the previous landlord, Jack, retired she had stayed on in charge at the behest of the brewery on a temporary basis, until they could appoint a new tenant. But tired of the nursing job she had done for years, she took on the tenancy herself and had made the temporary situation permanent.

Periodically through the evening she checked on her patient, he was sound asleep. After last orders and everyone had gone home, she locked up as usual and switched everything off in the bar and lounge. She went into her living room and sat on the armchair opposite Nick. It wasn't long before she too had drifted off.

Nick awoke at around three am. Looking around he did not recognise his surroundings at all. He took the towel from his head and wiped his face. As he focused he saw the landlady asleep on the chair and began to remember the night before. Quietly he stood up and folded the blanket. Reaching to put his shoes on he accidentally knocked the coffee table causing a glass to fall over which woke Barbara.

"Welcome back to the land of the living," she said with a hint of sarcasm and relief that he was OK.

"Yeah, sorry about that. I don't know what came over me, must be tired I guess," he excused.

"How are you feeling now?"

"Lousy. Any chance of a black coffee?"

"Expect you are hungry too?"

"Now that you come to mention it, I suppose it's been a while since I ate, but I don't want to put you to any trouble. You've done enough."

"No worries. Sit yourself down."

Barbara went to the kitchen and returned with two piping hot coffees and a plate full of ham sandwiches.

"Best I can do, it's the chef's night off," she joked.

"No, that's fine thankyou."

Nick devoured the food and emptied his coffee mug.

"Well thanks for that, I'd better get going and let you get some sleep."

"Go where? It's half past three in the morning for goodness sake, and it's freezing out there. Get yourself upstairs into bed you obviously need some rest," she invited.

"No honestly, I'll be alright I should go, I've put on you too much already."

"Nonsense! Who else have I got to look after? Even Jasper's abandoned me." She took Nick by the arm and said, "Come on I'll show you where the bathroom is."

Nick planted his feet firmly and said, "You are so very kind and I really do appreciate everything you've done, but I really do have to go now."

Barbara had quite a dejected look on her face and reached up stroking the back of Nick's head.

"Please stay."

Nicks emotions ran riot for a moment, then with a sigh he took hold of her hand. With his other hand he caressed her chin, pulling her gently towards him. He kissed her very briefly on the lips and said,

"Thanks ! Which is the way out?"

Reluctantly Barbara opened the back door and Nick stepped outside.

A last ditch attempt, Barbara said, "You are most welcome to stay you know," very temptingly.

"I know and I thankyou, but I have to go," he said very quietly, touched her cheek and walked away.

His love for Tanya and her precious memory was far too raw for him at the moment.

CHAPTER TWELVE

He walked through the empty streets back to his flat. Feeling a little wary of disturbing his pal Eric, he very quietly opened the door and removed his shoes before entering. As he took off his shoes he remembered Pete the feet and his philosophy on life. Taking it a stage further Nick removed his socks too. The cold paving slab felt refreshingly comfortable to the soles of his warm feet. "Nothing else matters," he recalled. "As long as I'm comfortable, then everything else is comfortable."

Nick felt very 'uncomfortable' about most of what had happened.

Pete's philosophy was that he started the day with a full cooked dinner of lamb chops, potatoes, vegetables and gravy, to set him up for the day. As the day wore on he may have a sandwich and if he was hungry late at night, he would have a bowl of cornflakes if 'bloomin necessary!'

His upside down world made Nick think about his own situation. His world had been turned upside down by events, whereas Pete chose to turn his life back to front, not conforming to the 'norm'.

To Nick the norm of life had gone forever.   Emotions in turmoil, Nick got into bed to recharge the batteries. Waking after a few hours and realising that it was Saturday, there was nothing he could do with regard to Aunty Joyce and her affairs, so his thoughts turned to young Carl in the homes, and the image of his face looking through the window, his open palm touching the glass.

Spruced up, he set off to visit him. On arrival at St. Christopher's Avenue he walked briskly to house number twelve and rapped on the knocker. After a few moments Mrs Forrester opened the door and asked, "Can I help you?"

Nick smiled, "Yes, I've come to see Carl."

"Oh, Right! Erm…." There was hesitation in her voice.

"Is there a problem?" enquired Nick

"No, no. Not at all!" she blustered, "I'm not sure if he's in at the moment."

"Not sure?"

"Well, I mean I haven't seen him for a while, since breakfast."

Uneasy with her excuses Nick said, "Well let's have a look then," and he stepped towards her.

Mrs Forrester, a wonderful carer for years of so many youngsters, had gradually been worn down by her dominant husband, whose behaviour had deteriorated more recently. She put on a brave face but inwardly she lived in fear for her own safety and more importantly the safety of her charges.

Nick could see anguish in her eyes and her whole demeanour seemed to show fear. He walked past her into the hallway and could hear a man's raised voice coming from the back garden. Hurrying through the house into the kitchen he looked through the window. On the lawn he saw Carl cowering on the ground with Mr Forrester shouting and waving his fist in the air above him.

Mrs Forrester had followed him and said, "It's ok really. He's just ticking him off for being naughty."

Nick raced out of the back door onto the lawn and stood a few feet away from them. "Stop!" he boomed.

Len Forrester froze. Slowly he turned to face the ex-marine standing erect, and with a fixed stare.

Carl lifted his head revealing a bandaged hand and wrist, and a plaster on his eyebrow. Seeing Nick again he jumped to his feet and ran towards him, grabbing him around the waist.

Nick touched his head and said, "It's ok now. Go inside with Mrs Forrester, I'll be in shortly."

Obediently Carl released his grip, looked up at Nick's face trustingly and slowly walked to the kitchen door. Len stretched to his full height, five foot four inches, and faced the intruder.

"It's you again! Poking your nose in," Len said aggressively.

"Yes it's me again. Now's the time to start running little man."

Belligerent Len launched a swinging punch towards Nick's head.

Calmly, Nick's larger hand engulfed the small mans first. With a twist, he turned Len's arm and reduced him to his knees. A sudden sharp yank produced a loud crack and Len's broken arm fell by his side. The dejected little chap cried out in agony and rolled onto his side.

Nick walked back into the kitchen. Carl was clutching Mrs Forrester's apron.

"It's all ok now," he reassured. "Get your things together. You are coming with me!"

Mrs Forrester said, "You can't do that!"

"Just watch me! You might need an ambulance for that little creep out there."

"What happened to Carl's hand?"

"Oh, he fell on it that's all," she lied.

"Really...? And what about the cut to his forehead?"

"Oh, that's just a small cut, an accident, nothing more," she insisted.

"That's exactly what just happened out there, a simple accident, he fell over, understand?"

Nick's forthright stare got the message across.

In a way Mrs Forrester was glad that at last someone had the courage to stand up to (or down to) her bullying husband even though she was still afraid of him.

Carl came bounding down the stairs with a bagful of clothes, his worldly possessions, feeling like an un-caged tiger. At last he was getting out of this horrible situation. He didn't care where he was going, just as long as it was away from Len's total dominance and cruelty.

Nick took Carl back to his flat reassuring him all the way that everything would be fine from now on. The young lad just felt very relieved, and pleased to be with his hero Nick. For two years he had endured brutality and indignation from the house master, with his wife tolerating the problem and concealing the truth from the inspectors and social workers to protect her husband, and preserve their jobs and house.

"What's going to happen to me?" he worriedly asked.

"First we're going to get you sorted and fed, then we'll see what needs to be done, but don't worry anymore, it'll be alright, I promise."

"Can I stay with you Nick?" he pleaded.

"For the moment, but then I'll have to sort out some permanent arrangements."

"So tell me what really happened to your wrist?"

"Oh that," Carl paused for a moment, "Len had given me a list of jobs to do and I hadn't completed them all when he came back from the pub, so he…."

"Go on."

"Well he held me by the wrist and gave me a Chinese burn, twisting his hands both ways. It really hurt and my wrist swelled, so Mrs Forrester put this bandage on for me."

Nick felt totally justified in his action earlier now, but wished he had inflicted a bit more suffering on that spineless little man.

"What about the cut on your forehead?"

"That was the day before."

"What happened?"

"I answered him back, that's against the rules so he hit me. His ring cut my eyebrow, but Mrs Forrester put this plaster on."

Thoughts of his own two lads came flooding back and the relatively calm life they had enjoyed.

Nick went into the bathroom and turned on the bath taps.

"Get yourself cleaned up, I'll go to the chippy and get us some lunch," he said, throwing a clean towel to the lad.

Nick needed a moment to compose himself. Stepping out into the cold November air, he lit a cigarette and tried to imagine the turmoil that Tud had gone through. Spending his time in constant fear was no way to live a life.

He walked to the chip shop to get their lunch, not sure what he was going to do with his new found charge, but at least certain that he was going to enjoy a much better life. After a fish and chip feast Nick suggested that Carl watched TV as he wanted to speak to his landlord about him staying in the flat for a while.

Downstairs Nick explained and asked Eric if he knew anyone in Social Services who he could speak to. As it happened one of his regular customers, Mrs Benson, who lived nearby, was a senior worker and he gave him her address. Nick paid her a visit and using all his persuasive charms got her to make several phone calls, even though her weekend off had been interrupted. Mrs Benson managed to find a placement in a foster home with a lovely family she had known for a long time, and who had successfully raised countless youngsters. The arrangement was for Nick to take Carl there on Sunday afternoon.

He and his young rescuee spent Saturday evening chatting and watching films on TV.

After breakfast Nick and Carl went for a walk. It was quite a crisp winter's day and the pair hurried along to keep warm. On their return Nick explained about the foster home plan, but Carl wasn't best pleased.

"But I thought I could stay here with you?"

"It's just not practical," Nick tried to reason. "This is just a temporary place for me to stay, and besides it's far too small. You will be much better off in a proper family environment."

To soften the blow slightly he gave Carl Aunty Joyce's mobile phone.

"Here's a present for you. Whenever you want to speak to me just press that button and it automatically rings my number."

After quite a lengthy chat, but with some reluctance, Carl agreed to go to his new home and stay with the Wilson family.

Arriving at the new address Carl was pleasantly surprised to see this rather imposing detached house with a huge front garden. Mrs Wilson, a fairly large lady, had a big smile and she welcomed them both in. The aroma of home-made cooking filled the air.

"Something smells good," said Nick.

"Oh that, I do all my own baking you know," she proudly pointed out.

She invited them into the front parlour. A rather grand room with a very high ceiling and large bay window fitted with red padded cushion seating. The three sat on the large sofa and Mrs Wilson, who insisted on being called by her first name, Nancy, explained the rules of the house.

She currently had two girls and one other boy staying with her all a similar age to Carl, but they were out at the cinema as a special treat, with her husband Wilf, a retired policeman.

"You will meet them all at tea time, which incidentally, will be served promptly at six pm in the dining room. Now let me show you which is your room," said Nancy getting to her feet.

"Well, I'll head off and leave you to it," said Nick.

"He'll be fine here with us, don't you fret about that."

"I'm sure he will. You have a lovely home."

Nick tucked a ten pound note into Carl's shirt pocket and said, "Get some credit on your phone. We'll chat tomorrow yeah?"

Carl nodded, feeling a bit too emotional to speak. Nick reached out and shook the youngster's hand.

"Be good for Mrs Wilson, sorry, I mean, Nancy."

Nick left promising to keep in touch.

The social worker Mrs Benson had said that she would be advising the inspectors about the problems at Carl's previous home and assured him that any necessary action would be taken as appropriate to safeguard the other children there.

Although Nick felt a little sad to be leaving Carl so soon, he knew that he was in the best possible place and with the court case and his Aunt's things to see to he would not have the time to look after him himself. He headed home to the flat and after some tea decided to phone his Aunt's neighbour about the possible sale of her bungalow. Still very keen Mr Armstrong said that he would contact his solicitor to get the ball rolling as soon as possible.

CHAPTER THIRTEEN

Attending his appointment promptly at 9.15am the po-faced receptionist apologised and said that Mr Bladen was not in. He hadn't phoned in sick or anything and that the practice was quite worried by this unusual non-attendance. Nick remembered her words from last Friday and asked, "What was the important case he was called away on?"

"Not sure," she said, "but he took a phone call on Friday afternoon and left the office at about 2pm. We've not heard from him since.

"Do you have a mobile number for him?"

"Yes, we've tried it several times, but the phone is switched off," she said.

"What about his home number?"

"No reply there either I'm afraid."

Perplexed and worried Nick wasn't sure what to make of this uncharacteristic disappearance. "I've got a court case on Wednesday!   I need to see someone, what about his partner?"

"Sorry, he's tied up at the moment with a client. If you would like to take a seat I'll see if he can fit you in," she obliged and closed the frosted window.

Nick paced up and down the small reception area wondering what was to become of the court case if his solicitor didn't show up. His gaze fixed on Steve Bladen's office door. Silently he tried the door. It wasn't locked. He entered and closed the door behind him. Scanning around the small office, searching for a clue, he rummaged through the brown files on his desk. Nothing apparent, to give any indication of where he might have gone. The waste paper basket was empty.

Nick sat in his chair trying to glean any piece of information he could. On the desk were two telephones, one had several lines, with extension names on it, from reception to his other colleagues in the building. The other was just a single phone. Nick picked it up and placed the handset by his ear. He could hear a dial tone. A long-shot, but he pressed 1471 and the operator's voice said, "Telephone number 01782 331331 called at 1.45pm on Friday 22nd November, to return the call press 3." He did, and it rang a few times before a woman's voice said tentatively, "Hello?"

Nick said, "Hello, who's that please?"

"I'm just a customer, but Joe's busy so I answered it for him."

"A customer where?"

"Joe's café on Broad Street," she said.

"Thankyou, I think I've got the wrong number." Said Nick and replaced the handset quietly.

He left the office and made his way to Broad Street as quickly as he could. The small café wasn't very busy. He approached the counter and asked for a coffee. Sitting on a bar stool he waited while Joe, the owner, served a customer. "Excuse me but I wonder if you can help me?"

Joe looked up from buttering some toast, "Yes what would you like?"

"No, nothing to eat. I need some information."

"Are you the police?"

"No!" assured Nick, but then, thinking to give himself some credence, said, "Not exactly."

"What then?" asked Joe.

"I'm investigating a missing person and trying to reunite him with his family. Can you recall last Friday afternoon?"

Joe gave the plate of toast to his patron and asked, "Last Friday you say?"

"Yes, perhaps around 2.30 or so, do you recall a little chap in a pin stripe suit coming in and possibly meeting someone here?"

"Now you mention it, yes. I remember the chap in the suit seemed very uneasy. He was fiddling with the cutlery and staring at the door. He nursed a coffee for about half an hour. Then two blokes came in and sat with him at that table in the corner. I asked them if they wanted anything but one of them, a German, I think, said no, they were leaving. At that the three of them left.... I thought it seemed a bit odd but we get allsorts in here you know."

"Thankyou. You've been very helpful," said Nick.

"That's Ok. Where did you say you were from?"

"I didn't," replied Nick, leaving the café.

Outside he was now even more intrigued about what had happened to Steve and just who were the mystery men?

He hurried back to the solicitors' office hoping he wasn't too late to see the partner. Nick entered the office and sat in reception just as a couple were leaving. The little window opened and the secretary said, "Mr Cheswardine will see you now."

Nick opened the office door and entered to see Steve's partner, a six footer in a tweed suit probably about sixty years of age.

"What can I do for you?" he asked.

"Steve Bladen is representing me in court on Wednesday but I can't get hold of him, do you know where he is?"

"No, not actually. We thought that he may be in late today but he hasn't turned in I'm afraid.

"So what happens to my case on Wednesday then?" Do you step in and take over or what?"

"I'm afraid it's not that simple. Steve is a litigation solicitor, whereas my speciality is house conveyancing. I'm sure that he will be in tomorrow.

Knowing that he had a strange rendezvous last Friday Nick asked, "What if he isn't in tomorrow."

"I really don't know what to tell you Mr Nixon. I suppose I could approach the court and ask for a postponement of the case, but I feel a bit reluctant to do that just at the moment."

Nick was undecided whether or not to tell him what he knew. He shook hands and left, arranging to ring in the morning. Worried what to do Nick paced the street for a while, and then had a change of heart and went back to tell Mr Cheswardine about last Friday's meeting at the cafe. The receptionist said he had left for the day. He had left through the back, to the staff car park. Nick decided to go to the police.

At the station he described everything he knew about Steve's disappearance to the duty Sergeant. The officer's face took on a very serious look. "Mr Nixon, I'm afraid I may well have some very bad news for you. We have recovered a body from the local canal, matching the detailed description you've given of Mr Bladen. As we understand it from his colleague at the practice he has recently divorced and now lived alone. We only got the dental record proof about an hour ago of his identity."

Nick's heart sank. As well as being so very sad about Steve, he wondered what was to become of the case against Vilner.

"What happened?" he asked.

"We are waiting for the post mortem results but at this stage it looks like a tragic accident."

"I don't think so Sergeant. I think you have a murder case on your hands."

"What makes you say that Mr Nixon?"

"The German. The meeting at the café. The court case. Put it all together man!"

"It's no use jumping to conclusions here."

"I'm not; I'm telling you that he was murdered. To shut him up. To stop the case." Nick said angrily.

"Let's get the post-mortem results first," said the sergeant, "then we will have a clearer idea of what happened."

Nick made a statement of what he knew and left the police station.

The next morning he phoned the solicitors and spoke to Mr Cheswardine, who had been informed of his partner's demise, to ask what was to happen. He said that The Crown would appoint a solicitor to present the prosecution case on Wednesday. With some trepidation he attended the court and his case was being presented by Mr Barrington-Adams, a crown appointed barrister.

The court case was very much a non-event. Evidence was presented such as it was, and the defence argument was so very strong that the judge directed the jury to find the defendant not guilty of dangerous or careless driving, but guilty of the much lesser charge of driving without due care and attention, and in view of the length of time he had spent in custody, should be released with a fine of five hundred pounds. He surmised that it was a tragic accident.

Nick could hardly believe his ears. He slammed his fists onto the desk and yelled at the judge. He was restrained by a policeman. His fixed glare at Vilner was full of hate. Vilner smirked back at him and was led down the steps to freedom. As he disappeared Nick scanned the courtroom. His body was shaking in total disbelief, he faltered, feeling that he was about to pass out, he grabbed at the desk to steady himself, experiencing an out of body feeling as though he wasn't really there.

He left the court in absolute shock. 'How the hell could this have happened?' The paltry fine seemed to devalue the lives of his wife and children. He could not believe that such a callous villain should be allowed to walk free. He lit a cigarette, inhaled deeply, and vowed to himself and to his family, that one day he would get even with Vilner.

CHAPTER FOURTEEN

An overwhelming feeling of dejection and betrayal engulfed Nick. He went to the off licence, bought a bottle and went back to his flat. Closing the door behind him he settled on the sofa with his alcoholic anaesthetic and a glass. It wasn't long before he drifted off into oblivion.

When he awoke several hours later he had a phone message on his mobile from Mr Cheswardine, asking him to ring the office regarding the offer he'd received from Mr Armstrong for his aunt's bungalow. He rang and accepted the offer, "Just get it done," he said.

"Completion should be in the next ten days."

"Fine, just do it."

What now he thought. What the heck am I going to do next. No job. No family. No home.

As he pondered, he remembered a poem his mother had given him years before. "Don't quit."

He recited it to himself having memorised it as a youngster.

(When things go wrong, as they sometimes will,
 When the road you're trudging seems all up hill.
When the funds are low, and the debts are high,
And you want to smile, but you have to sigh,
When care is pressing you down a bit,
Rest if you must, but don't you quit.)

Filled with resolve he showered and shaved and set off to find Vilner. From the original accident he recalled the name on Vilner's truck and the depot headquarters in Leeds. Arriving in Leeds he quickly found the depot and through the wire fence could see a dozen lorries all lined up in a neat row. Concealing himself behind a bush near to the fence, he patiently watched and waited. A loud tanoy announcement with a very distinctive female accent said, "Telephone call for Mr Goodwin," and repeated, filling the air on this otherwise quiet industrial estate.

Nick sat silently waiting, hoping to see Vilner, but as the hours passed he began to wonder whether this was the best approach. Around nine thirty or so, several cars began to arrive on the staff car park, presumably for the night shift. Nick's attention was revived. He watched carefully as the various different cars arrived and parked. Out of each one got a single male driver, each in turn going into the office for five minutes or so, then getting into a large artic and driving off into the night.

Just then a very old Mercedes pulled in and reversed into a space. The door opened and out stepped Vilner. He too went to the office and emerged to get into almost the last truck in the line. The lights came on and the lorry engine roared into life. Nick ran from his hiding place as fast as he could towards the main gate. The artic stopped at the barrier, Vilner got out and went into the office with

64

his release papers. Nick sneaked under the barrier and blindside of the office window, hurried to the back of the trailer. He unhooked two of the taut liner straps and climbed inside the back.

There was very little room, but he squeezed himself up onto the boxes and made a space pushing a couple of them to one side. The truck moved off and Nick settled expecting a long journey, but with no idea where to. After about an hour, the engine revs slowed and Nick could tell the lorry was pulling in somewhere, by the potholes. Sure enough the vehicle came to a halt, the air brakes hissed and the whole frame shuddered as the engine was switched off.

Quietly and carefully Nick crept down from his boxed perch to the small opening, He slipped out onto the lay-by and sneaked around the back to have a look. He could see Vilner standing at the front of the cab, illuminated slightly by the side lights he had left on. Two men approached from a parked V.W Golf and began a conversation. Nick edged a little closer hugging the wheels trying not to be seen or heard. He got within about five yards and could hear the three chatting away in German. Then he saw the tallest of the two pass a brown envelope to Vilner, who took it and put it under his jacket, in the inside pocket. The three shook hands and the two strangers walked back towards the V.W.

Nick retraced his steps quickly and climbed back through the opening. The truck started up and set off again. Nick pondered what the meeting was all about and what were the contents of the envelope? After several not very comfortable hours, the next sound Nick heard was that of a ship's horn. Peering through the hole under the tautlines he could see Dover signs. Crossing the channel was relatively smooth and pretty soon the lorry arrived in Amsterdam. Nick sneaked out of the trailer and hid nearby under a coach. Security guards with two Alsatians searched the lorry along with the rest in the line. Once they had cleared the row and begun down the second one, Nick climbed back in under the side cover and hid again in the boxes. The lorry rolled on and after about forty minutes it reversed into a loading bay to offload it's contents. Luckily the staff at the depot were on a break, and Nick slipped out and hid behind a low wall.

He saw Vilner exchanging papers in a wooden office and then go to the canteen. Patiently he kept silent, watching vigilantly, trying to suppress his stomach rumblings. He was starving and very thirsty.

A small army of men appeared and with almost military precision, they emptied the trailer with fork lifts in a matter of minutes. Similarly they then reloaded the trailer with yet more cargo, but halfway through, all the action suddenly stopped and all the staff disappeared back into the canteen.

Nick stared from his hiding place, his eyes flicking from side to side, trying not to miss a single movement. Vilner and another man appeared carrying a fairly large brown bag, and entered the back of the trailer. From his vantage point Nick couldn't see what they were doing.

After about fifteen minutes they both emerged, shook hands and parted. And, as if by a signal the depot workers re-appeared and finished loading the trailer.

Vilner strapped down all the sides and climbed into the cab. Nick rushed from his hiding place behind the wall and ran towards the lorry. He was moments too late as the artic began to move. Thinking quickly he ran alongside and jumped onto the plate between the cab and trailer. Holding on for his life's worth between the hydraulic couplings he gripped tightly to the swivel table, while the rig travelled at sixty miles an hour. He decided that rather than be in such a vulnerable position, he would be safer to climb up and try to get a better grip on the roof of the trailer.

Battling against the speed of the lorry with its consequent wind speed, his hunger and freezing cold, Nick grappled with the rigging and eventually heaved himself upon the top of the trailer. He worked his way along the cold wet tarpaulin roof and then felt a lump in the otherwise thin sheet. Fixing himself in a position holding onto a joint and pressing his feet against the solid roof side, he took out his Swiss army knife and cut a hole where the lump was. He pulled out blocks of what appeared to be drugs. Cutting further he discovered ten blocks, which had been hidden in the roof lining.

Bouncing around on the roof he tucked his jumper into his trousers and stuffed the packets inside. Clambering along the roof he came towards the back and clung on for dear life, hoping that the lorry would soon come to a stop. After what seemed like an age the rig ground to a halt. Nick waited and watched. Vilner had stopped next to a phone box, got out of the cab and made a call. Using his trusty knife, Nick cut a hole into the roof, just big enough to slip through and onto the boxes of cargo inside.

The truck pulled off again and arrived at Zeebrugge. Nick had fallen asleep, having thawed out a bit. Luckily there wasn't a security check at the port and Vilner's lorry boarded the cross channel ferry to Dover.

Back within sight of the white cliffs, Nick was aware that he could well be in very serious trouble if he was discovered with such a drugs haul in his possession. He stood on the boxes, slowly poked his head out of the hole in the roof and looked around the ferry deck. It was full of lorries and coaches. The starboard side of the ferry had a line of camper vans and motorhomes.

Nick waited until the ship had docked and all the drivers and passengers returned to their vehicles. He slipped out of the trailer and mingled along with the other passengers. As they all boarded their various vehicles Nick spotted a silver-haired couple getting into their motorhome. Stealthily he quietly opened the rear door and climbed in. Equipped with its own shower room Nick hid inside hoping that his unassuming, unknowing driver would not be stopped when they disembarked.

'Good call,' he thought to himself as the motorhome went straight through and out into the Kent countryside. He carefully opened the cubicle door and in the rear compartment he spotted a bowl of fruit. Feeling a bit cheeky he ate two banana's hoping that his host's wouldn't mind.

|The couple had been holidaying in Holland and had driven quite a distance that day, so feeling a bit weary they stopped at the services on the M2. Nick thought it prudent to jump out before his presence was noticed. He walked across the car park, dropped the banana skins into a waste bin and went into the services to take advantage of the washroom facilities.

Freshened up, he now had to find a way of getting back to the Potteries. He wandered around the lorry park looking for a Stoke based truck, and finding one he sat on the kerb and waited for the driver to return. Whilst waiting he packed the packs of drugs into his rucksack, not really certain what to do with them. His main aim was to get Vilner into trouble with whoever his suppliers and contacts were.

The driver came to his rig after his meal break and Nick asked if there was any chance of a lift back to Stoke. "I'm not really supposed to give lifts, it's all to do with the insurance," he said.

Stretching the truth a little, Nick said that he was a marine commando just back from Afghanistan and had lost his travel pass so was forced to hitchhike, and he had blown all his money on a belting good night out in Dover.

The driver took pity on him as he had a cousin serving out there, so agreed to give him a lift. Nick wasn't much company, sleeping for most of the journey. The driver woke him at Junction 16 and dropped him off in Stoke a short time later. He walked back to the flat and was relieved to close the door behind him. What a day. What to do now was the problem. Nick spent several hours thinking through the events of the last twenty four hours and the implications of the drug running operation he had intercepted.

CHAPTER FIFTEEN

Waking early as usual, Nick opened the rucksack and looked at the sealed bags of drugs wondering what their value might be, and what Vilner was going to do with them. Instinct told him to go to the police, but then how could he explain what had happened and would he be implicated in some way? Feeling so let down by the police and the court system, he resolved to take matters into his own hands and deal with Vilner himself. What to do with the drugs? He considered destroying them, but how? Then he thought he could somehow use the haul to destroy Vilner.

Thinking it through, he had seen Vilner accept an envelope probably containing cash for his part in smuggling the drugs into Britain. Vilner would then have had a serious problem explaining how he lost them. How often had he made such trips? Was the money being raised from their sale to fund the radical German cell that his brother Wilhelm belonged to, and their terrorist activities he was in prison for? Had Steve Bladen uncovered more at his café meeting and was he murdered to keep him silent?

There were so many ponderables.

He wondered whether he was going to be able to deal with it himself, or should he contact his ex marine pals for help. He agonised for a while but really didn't want to drag his mates into this potential mess. He refocused his mind on Vilner. He really wanted him dead by his own hands, not by some drug baron's or terrorist's. But he felt that he needed some insurance, some back up. All his marine training came back to him.

He knew now what he had to do.

This was going to be a real test of all his strengths and resources that he had honed to perfection over the last twelve years.

Showered and shaved he felt ready for the challenge.

First he wrote down a brief account of the drugs dealing and the location of where he was going to hide it, Vilner's involvement and the name and address on his truck in Leeds. He sealed the envelope and addressed it to Sgt Miller, the officer who had given him the tragic news of his family.

Next he got together everything he might need on his expedition. He took the blocks of drugs from his rucksack, packed them into a black bin bag and repacked them back into his rucksack. He went downstairs into the shop, and Eric was pleased to see him.

"How are you? We haven't seen much of you lately," he said.

"No, sorry about that, I've been pretty busy," he explained.

"Thanks for fixing the fence."

"No problem."

Nick had refitted Eric's fence which had blown down in the recent strong winds.

"Are you here for a while now?"

"Not sure, might just come and go for a bit if that's ok?"

"Of course, no problem Nick, is there anything I can do for you?"

"Actually you could help me out," Nick said quietly, then paused…No, it's ok. I'll be fine."

"Come on Nick, let me help, what can I do?"

Eric's enthusiasm boiled over, hoping he could do something to help his friend.

"I've just got a bit of a cash flow problem at the moment, but I should be getting a sizeable cheque pretty soon. You couldn't lend me a few quid till then could you?" Nick reluctantly asked.

"Of course, no problem, how much do you need?"

"A hundred quid would be handy if that's ok."

Eric went into his backroom, emerged moments later, and pressed a hundred and twenty pounds into Nick's hand.

"Thanks Eric, I will repay you very soon."

"Not at all, consider it payment for the fence," said Eric "Is there anything else I can do?"

"Well, now you come to mention it, are you using your car today?"

"No, it'll sit there all day while I'm in here."

Eric took the key from his pocket and gladly handed it to Nick.

"I'm really grateful to you," said Nick, shaking hands with his good friend.

Nick left the shop and loaded his stuff into Eric's car. His thoughts turned to young Carl at the foster home, and he felt that he should visit him before setting off to Leeds. He phoned Mrs Wilson (or Nancy as she insisted), and asked if it would be ok to visit. She most enthusiastically said yes and Carl would definitely be pleased to see him. Nancy promised to keep the visit a secret so that it would be a lovely surprise for him. He parked up and rang the doorbell.

Mrs Wilson was in the kitchen preparing food as usual and so asked Carl to answer the door. Willingly leaving his homework, he opened the front door. His face was a picture. A beaming smile from ear to ear, he grabbed Nick around the waist and sunk his head into Nick's chest. Instinctively Nick stroked the blonde hair on the back of his head.

"How ya doin fella?" he asked

"I'm doing fine, absolutely fine. It's wonderful here!" Carl exclaimed, "Come in."

The two of them went into the front parlour and settled on the sofa.

"What's this then? Homework from school?"

"Yeah, no problem, I'm doing a course on motor mechanics and have to hand this in on Monday as part of my assignment," Carl explained.

"Looks a bit complicated to me," said Nick

"No, it's not that bad really, once you get into it. Our teacher is very good, he explains all the workings and we have a model to practice on, so it all fits in."

Nancy came in from the kitchen with a tray of refreshments straight from the oven. The three of them had a good chat about Carl's progress and they all had a good feeling for his future. Also he got on very well with the other children and had taken quite a shine to Heather, a blonde sixteen year old who shared Carl's taste in music and had got Carl interested in swimming, a sport at which she excelled.

Nick was well pleased with the way Carl had settled in and was at last enjoying life, with goals and ambitions, not to mention a pretty young lady in tow. Mrs Wilson went back to preparing the evening meal, reassuringly patting Nick on his shoulder as she passed.

"I have something very important to say to you," said Nick to Carl.

Carl's facial expression changed, fearful of what he was about to be told, not wanting any more upheaval or change.

"I'm going away for a little while but I will be back."

Nick produced a hundred pounds from his pocket and taking Carl's hand he placed the notes into his fist.

"What's that for?" he asked

"It's just a chuffer," replied Nick.

"A chuffer, what's that?"

"It's just in case. A fallback. Keep it safe and if ever you need it, you know it's there."

He also took out his Swiss army knife and giving it to Carl said, "I want you to have this. It has served me well over the years, I've used it most days for something or other, as you can see from the wear marks. Perhaps it will come in handy for you too someday."

Carl was over the moon with his gift.

"I've always wanted one of these," he said happily, and he put it into his back pocket.

"So where are you going?" asked Carl worriedly.

"Oh, it's just a bit of business, not a problem, I'll soon have it sorted, don't worry."

Carl took in everything that Nick had said, but didn't really believe that all was ok. He trusted his hero completely but inwardly worried about him.

Nick said goodbye to Nancy and thanked her for her hospitality. Carl opened the front door, and the pair stood in the garden chatting for a while, completely unaware that they were being watched.

Vilner had returned to the lorry depot last night and discovered the drugs missing. His contacts were, to say the least, pretty angry that their consignment hadn't arrived. Vilner with the help of the security guard, had replayed the video tape from the camera covering the goods yard, and saw a good image of Nick near to his trailer before he'd set off for Amsterdam. For a reasonable sum, his corrupt solicitor had provided Nick's flat address from the court records. He had driven south from Leeds and followed Nick to the foster home. Nick and Carl shook hands as Nick went to Eric's car. He drove off and they waved to each other.

Vilner decided to let him go for now and sat watching the house, having witnessed the touching farewell. Nancy asked Carl if he would pop to the local shop to get some icing sugar for the cake she was baking. Dutifully he set off along the street to get it. Vilners old Mercedes quietly followed him and when he came out of the shop, sugar in hand, his accomplice grabbed him and bundled him into the back. Vilner put his foot down and they sped away. Now he had some bargaining power to retrieve the drugs. The bag of icing sugar lay in the gutter.

Nick had driven to the park, taken out a small rowing boat and rowed to the island in the middle of the lake, where he, Tanya and his lads had enjoyed such a great day before the tragedy. He moored the little boat, walked into the middle of the island, found a sheltered spot and buried the drugs, covering the area with leaves and a broken branch.

On his way to Leeds he posted the anonymous letter to Sgt Miller, thinking that the officer might gain some kudos from such a valuable drugs haul.

Nick found the depot at the industrial estate again, and parked nearby. He made his way to the perimeter fence and settled down in the bushes for what he anticipated could be quite a while. Several hours passed and although there was some movement of lorries in and out, none of the drivers were Vilner. Nick was quite cold and began to think that this was a futile exercise. He returned to the car and set off back to the Potteries, the heater soon had him thawed out, he stopped at a roadside café to get a drink, and some food.

Nick finished his coffee and back in the car was trying to work out how he would get hold of Vilner. As he started the engine his phone rang, so he switched it back off and took the phone from his pocket. The display said, TUD CALLING. He smiled and touched the green answer button to have a chat with Carl.

"Hi mate!" he said cheerfully.

There was no reply. Nick pressed the phone close to his ear and said, "Hello"

All he could hear was a crackling, muffled sound as though the phone was in a pocket or something. Nick listened hard hoping that Carl would speak or perhaps the signal would improve. Just then he could make out a tanoy announcement, "Mr Gooodwin please contact reception."

Nick knew that voice, he had heard it before, but where?

It rang out again repeating the same message. Racking his brains it suddenly dawned on him where he had heard it before, Vilner's depot.

But why was he hearing it on Carl's phone? He could only assume that he must have followed him to Leeds.

"Hello, hello!" he tried again but the line went dead.

Nick turned the key in the ignition, spun the car around and headed back to Leeds at speed.

CHAPTER SIXTEEN

At the depot Vilner and his accomplice Franz, had taken Carl into the warehouse, put him in the small office at the back, taped his mouth and bound his hands and feet with packaging tape. They then sat him in a chair and taped his legs to it. He was terrified, not knowing why these men had kidnapped him or what they intended to do to him. Secretly he had pressed the speed dial button on his mobile in his pocket, and hoped that somehow Nick could help

Nick neared the premises and coasted the car along the adjacent road then parked up. He quietly opened the boot and took out his rucksack, then made his way along the fence. Avoiding the camera he crept between the lorries and ran across the yard to the warehouse. He edged his way around the back and could see a small window about ten feet off the ground. Nick piled up a few pallets directly underneath and climbed on top to get a view inside. He peered through the dirty glass and in the corner could see Tud bound to the chair, with Vilner pacing up and down talking to Franz, their shapes more visible because of the white warehouse coats.

Now he understood the phone call. The last thing he wanted was the youngster mixed up in all of this. His eyes scanned the office. He could see the doorway and the steps leading down into the warehouse. He needed to draw them out somehow so that he could get to Tud. Nick climbed down, and crept along the side of the building to the front. He opened his rucksack, took out a balaclava, put it on and donned his gloves.

The main doors were open to receive the next delivery, so he sneaked inside and made his way along the edge, concealed by piles of boxes.   On the wall he spotted the fire alarm. He picked up a crow bar from the bench nearby and smashed the glass. The alarm bells rang out and the sprinkler system kicked in within seconds. The noise was quite deafening and the powerful water jets filled the air creating a mist throughout the warehouse. Two men who were working on fork lift trucks, ran outside and towards the main gate office.

Vilner and Franz, on hearing the bells, ran from the office shielding their eyes from the water and tried to see the fire that had caused this. Unable to detect any combustion the pair walked along the warehouse floor towards the main doors. Nick climbed into a fork lift truck, set it in motion towards the pair, gathering speed and raised the forks to about three feet off the ground.

Unaware of the approaching vehicle the two germans continued towards the opening. Nick steered the machine at Franz, the forks hitting him in the back and pinning him against the wall, adjacent to the doorway. The crash threw Nick off and he fell on the soaking floor injuring his left arm in the process.

Vilner saw his pal in a mess trapped against the wall and assumed him to be dead. He pulled a gun from his inside pocket and ran into the yard, not really sure what was going on. Nick scrambled to his feet, shrugging off the pain in his arm and followed him outside. Vilner heard footsteps, turned and raised his gun, holding it with both hands he pointed it at Nick and cocked the hammer. Staring at the barrel Nick stood still.

"You have caused me a lot of trouble," Vilner said in his german accent, "Give me back the drugs and you can have the boy."

"I've caused you some trouble! That's rich!." Nick defiantly retorted. The two adversaries squared up to each other about twenty feet apart.

In the meantime Tud, now free from his captors, reached into his back pocket, his fingertips just managing to get a purchase onto the swiss army knife. Behind his back, fumbling, his finger nail caught on one of the recesses and he was able to prize open a blade. Nick had always kept them razor sharp, so it quickly cut through the tape binding his wrists. His hands free he was able to reach down and cut the tape wrapped around his ankles. He peeled the tape from his mouth, it stung a bit and he felt really thirsty.

Unsure of what to do, he slowly walked down the office steps into the now soaking wet warehouse. Dry as a bone, he tilted his head back and open mouthed, drank in the cold watery spray. Refreshed but still bewildered and wishing his hero was here he crept along the pallets of boxes through the mist. He reached the open door and hid behind the recess not knowing whether to make a run for it or stay put. He peered around the opening and could see Nick standing facing the pointed gun Vilner was aiming at him.

In panic he ran out and shouted at the top of his voice, "Leave him alone!" Vilner, shocked at this intrusion and amazed to see the lad free, turned the gun towards him. Tud dodged back into the warehouse behind the opening just as Vilner fired his gun, the bullet ricocheting off the metal frame.

Quick as a flash Nick rolled onto the ground and away to his right behind one of the lorries. Blinded slightly by the flash from the gunshot Vilner regained his focus and looked around for Nick. The yard was bare, only a row of lorries and an eerie silence. He knew he was up against a formidable adversary and needed to take cover, so he ran back into the warehouse.

Once inside he could see that the sprinkler system was in full flow, and the alarm bells were still ringing. Tud saw him gun in hand and ran away along the warehouse. Vilner ran after him and slid along the wet floor taking Tud down grabbing him around the throat.

The pair came to a halt hitting some of the boxes. Vilner climbed on top of the young lad, still holding his throat and pointed the gun at his temple. Feeling reassured he was now in total control he yelled out.

"Come on marine! Let's get it on! I've got your precious boy. Let's trade."

Fire engine sirens now filled the air, the company alarm system had alerted the local station when it went off. Three appliances raced to the scene with blue lights illuminating the warehouse. Nick had run back to the outside window, opened his rucksack and took out a large bladed knife, climbed the pallets and using the blade forced open the window. Through the small opening he climbed into the office as silently as a ninja. He looked from the office into the warehouse and through the watery haze could see Vilner holding Tud with the gun pressed to his head.

Suddenly the alarm stopped and the sprinklers died down. The noise was replaced by the sirens from the fire engines. Nick knew that he had to act fast, before too many people clouded things. He walked down the steps onto the warehouse floor and yelled.

"Release the boy!"

Vilner shouted back, "Show yourself, give me the drugs and you can have him."

Nick moved nearer to them, held his hands in the air and said,

"Release the boy. Let him go and you can have the drugs."

"Why should I believe you? I've got your precious boy, where are the drugs?"

"I've got them in my car just outside the yard. Let him go and I'll take you to them," Nick bargained.

Vilner tightened his grip on Tud and turned him around. With his other hand he took a grip on his arm and bent it behind his back.

"I'll break his arm. You know I will. Go and get the drugs, bring them here now, then you can have him," sneered Vilner.

"Ok, ok. Don't harm him. I'll do as you say. Give me a minute. I need to use my chuffer.

Perplexed Vilner asked, "What is a chuffer?"

Tud realised Nick was giving him a signal, he reached into his pocket with his free hand and his fingers gripped the swiss army knife. Opening the blade he swung it with all his might into Vilner's thigh. The blade sank into his flesh with an almighty crunch and Vilner yelled out in pain, fell to the ground, releasing his grip on Tud, and dropping his gun.

"Run!" Nick yelled.

Tud leapt to his feet and moved away from Vilner. Nick ran to the stricken German and placed his hand around his throat, sitting on top of him. His blood rushing through his veins, he pictured Tanya and his two boys. His grip tightened, Vilner began to choke and his eyes started to bulge. Nick stared into his eyes, exploring his soul. Vilner looked back in total defiance. Digging deep Vilner launched a last ditch blow towards Nick's left arm. The pain was almost unbearable and Nick fell off his quarry onto the wet floor. His arm was obviously broken and numbness travelled from his shoulder to his fingers.

Vilner picked himself up and grabbed Tud, who had been frozen to the spot watching them. He picked him up and ran out of the warehouse. Nick, his arm dangling useless by his side, got to his feet and staggered towards the doorway. The fire engines arrived. Their sirens stopped.

Nick emerged and leaned up against the outside wall looking for Vilner and Tud. He saw movement under the trailer of one of the lorries and stealthily moved towards it. As he rounded the cab he could see Vilner on top of Tud, hitting him in the face. Memories of the garden where he had encountered the housemaster beating down on him flooded back. He ran at Vilner and took him with a tackle his ex-marine mates would have been proud of. The two of them rolled along the tarmac, Nick landing on top of Vilner. Tud ran off into the warehouse and took refuge by the workbench.

Nick started to hit Vilner in the face, his blows from his right hand smashing the man's nose and teeth. Nick rained the blows towards his face releasing all the anger that had built up over the months. Each blow had a reason. One for Tanya. One for Tony. One for Craig.

Vilner lay quite limp. Nick thought he had probably killed him. The realisation of such an act by his own bare hands made him shudder.

But he was glad. Revenge is sweet.

He rolled off onto the ground and the pain from his broken arm brought him back to reality. Where was Tud? Was he Ok?

Just then Vilner rose up off the ground, hit Nick on the back, and stamped on his head.

Laughing he said, "You can't beat me Englishman!"

He kicked Nick in the ribs and got him around the throat.

"Where are my drugs you little piece of shit?"

"You will never know, you will die not knowing," Nick defied.

Tud had spotted a pair of mole grips on the bench and went to one of the tractor units in the line. Using his acquired skills, he released the brake pipes on the unit. The machine hissed and surged forward.

Gathering momentum the lorry sped along the park out of control. Nick and Vilner were still grappling with each other. Vilner hit out and Nick reeled back onto the ground. Vilner stood over Nick sneering at him, the same look he had given in the court, blood dripping from his battered face.

Silently the tractor unit ran towards them. Oblivious to the imminent danger, Vilner looked pleased with himself and glared at Nick thinking he had got the better of him. Nick, lying prostrate, with a broken arm, heard Tud shout, "Eyes right!", then saw the oncoming flat fronted rig racing towards them, and quickly rolled to the side. The truck hit Vilner, knocking him to the ground, and the wheels ran over his body crushing the very life out of him. The lorry crashed into the fence and stopped.

CHAPTER SEVENTEEN

The fire crews were racing around the warehouse looking for the seat of the fire to no avail.

Nick looked at Vilner's crushed body and an overwhelming sense of justice filled his mind. 'Live by the sword, die by the sword' he thought.

Tud ran to Nick, his lip bleeding quite badly, and asked, "Are you Ok?"

Nick said, "Yeah, I'm fine. Thanks for the shout, how are you?"

Tud spat some blood to the ground and said, "Ok, I think. Who the heck was that man?"

"A nobody, just a nobody. Let's get out of here.

Run to the car over there past the fence, in the street, a little blue Toyota, I'll catch up in a minute."

Tud obediently ran off the site, wiping his mouth on his sleeve.

Nick took a last lingering look at Vilner's corpse lying on the cold, wet tarmac, his blood ebbing away into the gutter at the edge of the pound.

He had mixed emotions. Extremely glad that he was dead and by the wheels of a truck, the very way in which his family had been so tragically wiped out. But strangely sad, that his quest was now over.

Part of him wanted to kick him one last time, but he resisted the urge.

"Come on!" yelled Tud from the car.

His voice brought Nick back to reality, he looked around, then saw the bright blue light of the fire engines, felt the awful pain in his arm and shoulder and moved towards Tud's voice.

A shot rang out. A searing pain surged through Nick's right arm. Blood began to run down his sleeve. He looked from where the flash had come. Near to the entrance of the warehouse he could see Franz sitting with his arms outstretched and a gun held in his hands pointing towards Nick. He had released himself from the forklift.

Nick fell to the ground next to Vilner. He spotted a knife handle sticking out of his pocket. Nick took hold and pulled out a seven inch knife. He hurled the weapon with all of his might, ignoring the pain in his arm. With deadly accuracy the blade embedded itself into Franz's chest, bringing his sad evil life to an abrupt end.

He picked himself up and walked with some difficulty towards the car. Police cars began to arrive at the depot, sirens and flashing lights illuminating the darkness. Tud was waiting by the car, even more frightened now by hearing the gunshot. Nick staggered through a gap in the fence and opened the car door. He slumped into the driver's seat and put the key in the ignition. Eric's little car sprang into life, Tud jumped into the passenger seat and the pair raced off away from the area.

Nick's injuries were really painful making driving too difficult. His left arm was broken and he had a bullet wound in his right upper forearm. About a mile road he stopped the car and said, "You are going to have to change gear, I can't."

"You're bleeding!" Tud shouted.

"Yeah, don't worry, just change gear when I tell you." Nick feeling quite weak, took a cigarette out of his packet, just managed to place it between his lips and using Pete the feet's lighter, lit the end of his comfort stick. Inhaling deeply, he knew that he had to get Tud out of this situation.

He opened the window and began to drive, explaining to Tud how to manoeuvre the gear stick. The blood from his wound continued to flow and Nick became increasingly weak. He drove to Leeds railway station with Tud's help, they parked near to the taxi rank, and Nick asked Tud to check if there were any trains going south. The last train had gone and the station was about to close. Fearing that he just couldn't drive any further Nick said, "I'm done, I need to sleep."

Tud put his hands around his neck and gently shook him, "Come on mate, let's get a taxi," he suggested.

"I can't afford it"

Tud produced a wad of cash, "But I can."

On the rank was a sole taxi, hopeful of a last fare before he called it a night. The pair boarded the taxi and asked if he fancied a trip to Stoke. The driver said he didn't mind, but could they pay a deposit. Tud produced his chuffer and gave the driver forty pounds. "Will that do?" he enquired and smiled at Nick.

The driver set off south, not noticing Nicks injuries, only too pleased to rescue what had been a very quiet evening. On the way Nick removed his jacket with Tuds help and instructed the lad to cut the sleeves into strips with his swiss army knife. They used some as padding and some to bind the wound in his arm. As they neared Nick's home he asked the driver to drop them off, not wanting to give the driver any information of where they were staying. Tud paid the driver his fare and the black cab disappeared down the road.

The pair wandered along the street, helping each other to stay upright. Nick's bleeding had abated and Tud's lip had scabbed over. They came to the steps that led down to the towpath, so they descended and walked along the canal towards Nick's flat.

As they passed the lock where they had first met, very quietly and unnoticed by Nick, Tud took the mole grips from his pocket and dropped them into the water with a plop.

Nick relied on Tud's strength and with his arm around his shoulder they managed to make progress towards Nick's flat. When they arrived Nick said, "Take the key from my pocket and let us in as quietly as you can." Tud opened the door and supported Nick up the stairs.

He collapsed onto the bed exhausted and very weak from the pain in his broken arm, and the blood loss. Tud wasn't sure what to do, he got a towel and soaked it under the tap, placed it on Nick's forehead, held his hand contemplated phoning for an ambulance. Nick opened his eyes and said, "Go home. I'm fine honestly, it's only a little wound. I'll deal with it. Go home, I'll see you tomorrow."

Tud knew Nick's resolve and strength, but still worried about his hero.

"Go on, I'm ok. A few hour's kip and I'll be fine," he reassured him, "the bullet went straight through, I'll be right as rain pretty soon."

"But what was it all about? Who were those men? Why did they kidnap me.

"Don't worry, It's all over now. They are gone. I'll explain it all to you tomorrow," Nick sighed and turned his head to the side, to sleep.

Tud left, and returned to his foster home apologising profusely to Nancy about the icing sugar, pretending he had met a mate and they had gone to the cinema and lost track of time. She was fine about it, but had been quite worried. She asked about his lip and he explained that he had walked into a lamp-post while chatting to his mate.

Nick drifted off into a deep sleep. He dreamt the headline in the newspapers read, 'Feuding drugs dealers kill each other' and a sub-story of Sgt Miller receiving praise for finding a drugs haul with an estimated street value of half a million pounds.

He dreamt that he had received the cheque from his solicitors for the sale of his aunt's house and bought a leasehold on a chocolate box style country inn, nestling in a pretty Derbyshire village with a stream running alongside the beer garden. In his dream, Tud had left the foster home and come to work with him in the pub. Landlady Barbara had sold her tenancy and come to help out too, living in the annexe. All three were having a fabulous evening laughing and joking with the regulars when the bitter ran out.

"No problem" said Nick, "I'll pop down the cellar and change the barrel."

He disappeared down the steps behind the bar to connect a fresh supply. The cellar was quite small and had a very low ceiling, causing anyone entering to stoop, avoiding a head collision with the beams, a brass plaque proclaimed, 'Duck or Grouse.'

Nick head butted the hundred watt light bulb sending it swinging from side to side, illuminating the dark recesses then plunging them back into darkness. His pupils really struggled with the penetrating light and he passed out on the steps.

Waking, in what seemed like seconds later, the same bright light was piercing his eyes. Slowly, as his focus sharpened from a blur, he was confronted by a doctor, all in white, who was shining a medical torch into his eyes.

Doctor Klaus Vilner an eminent German doctor and skilled field surgeon, had been treating Nick for the last two weeks and monitoring his condition, while he had been in a coma in the military hospital, induced by the severe blood loss he'd suffered on the way back from the battle he and his comrades had endured with the insurgents.

Turning his head to the side he could see a photograph of Tanya and his boys on the bedside cabinet, put there by Arthur for when he woke up, along with several unopened letters from them. On top of the pile was a letter he had received about three weeks before, which he had read from Carl (or Tud as he was later to be known), requesting a marine pen pal.

His school had formulated the idea of writing to serving force personnel in Iraq and Afghanistan in the hope of fostering a better understanding of the conflict and maybe forging some friendships. Nick had read Tud's letter, and was touched by the lads honesty and sincerity. He was being brought up in a foster home and longed for the day when he was old enough to join the marines. Nick had intended to reply, but hadn't yet.

Looking around the makeshift ward, he could see other soldiers and marines in beds with various bandaging and drips attached. The doctor, Klaus Vilner, gave him a sip of water. Nick swallowed.

It was the first liquid to pass down his throat for two weeks. I felt good.

Confused he could hardly believe that Vilner was there, caring for him. He drifted in and out of consciousness for several minutes.

When he came to again, he looked across the room trying to make some sense of the situation. In the corner, large as life was Arthur (the fixer) sitting reading a book.

In his croaky voice that he hadn't used for two weeks he called, "Arthur..."

Putting his book down Arthur looked at Nick and said, "Welcome back me old mate, I thought you were going to sleep forever! Once we're fit and the doc's let us out of here we'll be back in dear old blighty eh?"

Nick nodded, still struggling to make sense of everything.

"Taff and the Prince went home last Monday," Arthur added, the Prince had an appointment with his solicitor about something, and Taff was going on about running his mate's pub in Derbyshire while he was on holiday." On the bedside cabinet next to Arthur was a bowl of fruit with bananas on the top.

Nick began to realize that he was still here in Afghanistan. His heart sank.

But were his family ok? Were Joyce and Bladen ok?

He looked up at Dr. Vilner and asked, "Why do I feel so dreadful? What's happened to me?"

"It's probably the drugs. You've had a lorry load to alleviate the pain," he explained placing his fingers on Nick's throat to feel his pulse.

His colleague, Dr. Franz Houseman, adjusted the drip above Nick's bed and said, "I'll order some more saline from the warehouse."

Arthur, recovering from his shattered leg shouted across enthusiastically, "When we are declared fit to travel and get the hell out of here, settle back at home for a while, I'll give you a ring and we four can have a get together if you like?"

Nick began to sweat.

"No please don't," he said quietly, and with some relief, drifted back off into his world of collisions.

Printed in Great Britain
by Amazon